DOMINATED

CW00498173

DOMINATED BY THE HEIR

First edition. February 11, 2024.

ISBN: 979-8224359004

Written by Maebel Credence.

Table of Contents

Chapter One: The Heir..1

Chapter Two: Slave 6

Chapter Three: Obey Me...12

Chapter Four: Pretty Little Mouth 16

Chapter Five: Punishment Deserved 20

Chapter Six: Work For It...24

Chapter Seven: Inappropriate Relations 28

Chapter Eight: A Valuable Lesson 31

Chapter Nine: Wait 35

Chapter Ten: A Slight Improvement 39

Chapter Eleven: Clamped 42

Chapter Twelve: Setting Up..45

Chapter Thirteen: Self-control..48

Chapter Fourteen: Rewards 53

Chapter Fifteen: Table Time...57

Chapter Sixteen: Another Chance 60

Chapter Seventeen: Relax..65

Chapter Eighteen: Wonderful Things 69

Chapter Nineteen: Do You Like It 73

Chapter Twenty: The Master...77

Chapter One: The Heir

The heir had the sort of dominant stare that, though menacing, could drench any woman's panties. I'd noticed it the first time I saw him at his father's home, where I lived during my summer breaks from university. The six-foot-four man was probably in his late twenties at that time. And the scalding look he'd cast my way on a few occasions suggested his repulsion of my mother and me living with his father.

I'd only heard him speak once, and his cold words of detest for my gold-digging mother resonated, and, of the few times I would have seen him afterward, I preferred to remain in my room. At this point, I didn't even remember his name.

The last time I saw the asshole had been at his father's funeral a week ago. Even then, the dead man's sole son had been absurdly handsome—looking like power divine with the intensity of how he watched me. But now, standing in my apartment, he bore a new stare and set of his jaw that warned of his intention to intimidate. And even in the casual jeans and fitted gray tee, he was still just as attractive as the suit that had me taking second glances in his direction during the funeral.

On to the issue at hand, why the fuck was this prick standing inside my apartment bearing the stony expression I knew not to fuck with? Maybe a better question would be why I didn't run outside, given how much I feared his dark brown gaze that had held contempt for me on more than one occasion.

"Shut the door," he ordered from where he leaned against the wall. And he didn't have the sort of voice a woman would dare ignore. That dreadfully dominant tone was part of why I'd gone to my room the few times he'd visited his father while me and my mother lived with him.

I obeyed, guiding the door closed silently.

"Lock it," he demanded, not bothering to push back the brown hair that fell just past his brow.

"I think you have the wrong apartment." My voice came out sheepish, childish even. I knew better than to piss off the arrogant son of my mother's dead lover.

"My father's name is on the lease." His hand glided over a portrait of me and my boyfriend that hung on the wall. "That makes this *my* luxury apartment."

I took in a deep breath. "Oh."

That wouldn't go over too well. Mom never was good at reminding me of such things. I would need to figure out something else while she sorted things out.

I locked the door as he'd previously ordered, certain this man came to insult my mother for whatever she may have received from the wealthy man's estate. And this last lover of hers had more than a few million to fight over. I'd been bullied before by people who felt my mother deserved no more than to be spit on, so this was nothing new.

"Sit," he ordered. The word came out as though I was nothing more than a dog.

Again, nothing new to the insults. Just let him fume so he would leave. If necessary, I could find other arrangements.

I went to the small round table, intentionally sitting with my back to the dominant man. It would be my one passive-aggressive act that forced him to move in order to take control of the situation.

"If your slut mom is half as obedient as you, I see why my father kept her around." As he spoke, his voice grew closer until he stood against my upper back.

The heir's hand curled around my throat, most likely in warning for me not to mouth off. Not that I considered doing so. He'd terrified me plenty without words the few previous occasions I saw him.

"What are you willing to do to ensure you get to graduate next month, and I don't toss out all of your belongings or have a chat with a few professors?"

My swallow strained against his grip on my throat. I'd never been asked anything like that either. Was he demanding I fuck him so I got to graduate? Shamefully, it had heat blooming within me. Now I wondered if he'd wanted to do this before. To treat me as men treated my mother.

His left hand reached down to my breast, this touch causing me to squirm from the embarrassing violation. His hold on my neck didn't budge, though.

The worst part of this encounter was how my body reacted to him. He turned me on with that dark and brooding demeanor. It wasn't something I could help. I loathed him. Despite that, the thought of being rutted by him sent the sort of catch to my breath that his palm currently clasping my breast could feel. And I'd hated the secret heat he'd caused on the few times his glare had landed on me from afar.

His grip beneath my chin tilted my head upward to look at him. That soul-consuming brown stare captured me again. My mom would know how to handle the situation were she in this chair, but I wouldn't humiliate myself by attempting her level of seduction. Instead of her incessant desire for such a dominating man, I feared what might happen. And he must have known as he searched every detail of my uneasy response to him.

His groping hand went to the neckline of my shirt, yanking it and my bra downward. Would this man, whose name I still didn't recall, decide he wanted to do more than threaten me?

"What are you asking for?" I asked, trying to sound as though I could hold my own in this confrontation if need be.

The hand around my neck loosened before roving over my shoulder. "You already know what you need to do." His tongue wet his lips as he prepared to devour me.

And I did already know what was expected of me. I turned in the seat to face him, before lowering my knees to the carpet. That long lock of his hair swooped forward as his face tilted to watch. I hadn't done anything yet, but the forceful grip he placed on the back of my head warned that he owned my face for the time being.

"Unclasp my jeans." He spoke with an authority that I had no will to refuse. The swell in front of my face already had the pants so tight it was hard to grip the area.

I had second guesses on whether or not I wanted to do this. I hadn't seen it yet but felt certain the size of his cock would prove unpleasant once he thoroughly used me with it. The palm that held my head in place ensured me there would be no opportunity to change my mind.

I fumbled, finally unclasping the pants and pulling them down for his cock to spring out and thwack my cheek. The moment I gripped it, he let out a deep, quick exhale. Maybe the millionaire heir hadn't cum in a while. If so, this could be quick and easy.

"Open your mouth, already!" he said, a little too eager for this.

At the command, my lips parted, and I leaned forward to lick the swollen tip. I wondered if he'd been wanting me to do this at the funeral as he'd leered at me in the same way. Or any other time before that.

I forced my mouth to open wide to take him in. He may have been more than eager to have me do this, but I couldn't rely on his hips pumping to speed up the process. I had to wrap my lips around him and do all the work, bobbing my head, squeezing, sucking, tasting the salty pre-cum, creating a soreness in my jaw as I pleased him.

"You have no fucking idea what you're doing, do you, little slut?" he said haughtily. With that ridicule came a thrust of his hips that rammed his cock deep into my throat so far that I felt as though I'd gag. His hold hindered my ability to pull backward.

Some women might have stopped after the insult and excessive force. I should have been one of those self-respecting women, but maybe I needed to rationalize what I'd chosen to do in order to finish university without issue.

"If you hadn't been such a bitch, I would have already made sure you knew what you were doing." With every exaggerated pump, he glared down as though he owned me. As though he needed to punish me for years of refusing to be in his presence. As though I needed to thank him every time he pulled all the way out, so I had a chance to breathe — not that he gave me that luxury too often.

His fingertips dug into my scalp, silently asserting their own dominance as he held himself deep. He could've simply fucked my face and been done, but he preferred the long enduring ownership of me. Something he'd apparently wanted for a while.

"You should know," he said with an exceptionally deep pump, "I never cum during a blow job."

He didn't stop, though; he simply made me realize this had nothing to do with his own physical pleasure. Of course, with a cock that big, he needed free rein somewhere without teeth. I'd never had anything larger than five and a half inches in me, not to mention the added girth he sported.

When it became obvious that this was a game to him, I finally jerked my head free. "Just fuck me already. It seems you've wanted to long enough," I panted.

I could already feel the unwelcome drenching of my panties, anyway. I may not have wanted something that huge inside me under normal circumstances, but he had my being ever-increasingly craving release during this shameful session.

His eyes narrowed. "But I'm having fun."

My sore jaw clenched at his mockery.

He pushed my head to the side. "Take off your clothes and crawl on hands and knees to your bedroom, so that pussy of yours earns every penny of rent and tuition."

Chapter Two: Slave

I didn't immediately respond to his order to strip and crawl. I wasn't certain how to respond. It was one more month. That was all I needed in order to graduate and move on.

Should I obey? Take off my clothes? Crawl on hands and knees?

Surely, he couldn't be serious. My choice to give him a blow job was meant to be a quick act to satisfy him into letting me stay until I got my diploma. Preferably longer, but I didn't plan to make any requests or be paid another visit from him.

"Over one hundred-K of what should have been my inheritance was spent on your college, and I'm not going to continue to dish out money for your life of luxury unless you fucking earn it."

Heat bubbled within me further. It shouldn't have. I should have been repulsed by his expectation.

I'd dated a few bullying jerks, but this man's threatening seemed different. In control, unwavering, and one-hundred percent Alpha in an unbelievable way.

I remained on my knees as I wiggled out of my shoes, then my dress. For some reason, I felt entranced by his eyes; one hidden behind that unruly, dark clump of hair that hung forward. He held that stare right up until my nude bra came off. Once that happened, he set his judging interests on my B cup breasts. His expression told me nothing about whether or not he liked what he saw. Most likely, he didn't.

All that remained were my red panties. It was a bit embarrassing for such a powerful man to see me in unmatched underwear. At least I'd waxed for my upcoming date. The thought made me realize I probably had only a few hours to make sure this prick left my — now his — luxury apartment. Hopefully, he didn't have too much endurance to fuck me for very long.

Still on my knees, I wiggled the underwear down, then kicked them off; suddenly uncomfortable with the roving eyes that lingered even longer on my bare cunt.

His dick still angled toward my face, hard and ready to fuck my mouth or any other hole it had the opportunity to have.

"To your bed, little slut." His continued use of the insult agitated me. Men had good reason to call my mom a slut, but not me.

My face lowered, hiding my irritation. "I've only fucked one man, so the least you can do is stop calling me a slut."

His responding expression held a flash of cruelty. "My dick is the only one you'll have from now on. Now drop to your hands and knees and get to your bed."

From now on? He wouldn't own my body for any longer than today. Possibly a few other times before graduation, but nothing more.

I obeyed his hostile command and lowered my palms to the carpet. He would see me in a way I'd never permitted anyone to. As I took the moment to gather my courage and move forward so he could watch me in this embarrassing position, a pain landed so hard on my backside, I almost fell forward.

"Don't ever mention another man again," he explained, still hung on the issue of my boyfriend. The hand that spanked me lowered to glide the full length of my folds with a warning tap. "Move it!"

Again, I obeyed, this time without hesitation, given how much my rear still stung. I didn't move too fast. That would look even more silly. I already imagined how pinkened the mark to my backside must have been.

When I looked over my shoulder to see where he was, another hard spanking landed against my other cheek. His hand remained at the spot when I stiffened. I only blinked away the tears of pain. The bastard intended to make me suffer in order to finish college. Would he do this for the next month? I'd assumed today would suffice.

After the moment of shock, I quickened my pace, careful not to hurt my knees. The long, miserable crawl held the terror of another spanking possibly coming for any misstep. Luckily, it didn't.

When I reached the door, he leaned over me and pushed it open. The thought that he'd been here long enough to know the details of my home also worried me. I refused to act on my desire to call him out on invading my privacy. That might end in more pain.

Once near my bed, I attempted to stand before his hand landed on my shoulder, blocking me from rising beyond upright on my knees.

"I didn't give you permission to stand, slave."

The new name he chose to call me felt only slightly better than slut. Did I say anything in rebuttal, though? Of course not. He'd probably wanted to call me that for years.

Still on my knees with my body upright, I remained frozen to the spot, catching his swaying manhood in my periphery. How the fuck would I be able to handle that massive thing?

His fingertips went to my left nipple, circling it. At my quiver, he said, "That's a good girl. You like this, don't you?"

It was too surprising in comparison to what I expected of him. The ever-increasing throb that built between my legs couldn't be ignored. Of all he'd done thus far, nothing had me as riled as the way that praise, combined with the touch to my breast, felt. It may have been embarrassing to admit, but I had no doubt he already knew I liked it. "Yes."

"Yes," he said, "Master." He didn't have to directly tell me to call him that. I knew some bits about this fetish rich men had. This was the cost of my education. It would need to seem genuine.

The hard pinch he added pulled me from my reverie. "Answer correctly."

"Yes, Master," I whimpered.

The firm hold to my nipple freed. "Stand up, slave," he snapped.

I rose, cautiously looking at the bed that had been made. He must have made it. The white comforter and pillows appeared as smooth as a hotel would. But a hotel wouldn't have strings of rope or what appeared to be a collar at the far side of the queen-sized mattress.

I remained in place, questioning whether I could handle this new day he expected of me. Considering the situation further, I doubted my mother would give me anything in help for the predicament. She would tell me to use my natural assets, most likely. Or she might even mention seducing this heir in order to ensure she got something out of the death of an old man who never married her.

"We're going to need a bigger bed, but this will have to do for now." *We?* His declaration said way too much about his plans regarding me over the next month. With a palm at my lower back, he directed me to the center at the end of the mattress. "Lean over the edge, so I can see how wet your cunt has always been at the thought of me."

Assholes riled my body. It had nothing to do with him personally. Even during rages, my boyfriend's insults turned me on.

I bent forward, knowing better than to say a word. The man may not even let me say no, now that things had progressed this far.

His fingers slid too easily in the slickness between my folds, reaching my aching nub. The gasp he elicited from me received his responding chuckle. "It didn't take you long at all to glisten for me."

He leaned his body onto mine, firm chest to my back, and cock rubbing the length of my slit. With one hand braced beside my head, he fisted my hair and guided my head up. His tone held warning as he spoke close to my ear. "And your cunt is for only me! Right, slave?"

His expectations became cemented in my psyche. Obedient and catering to his ego, all so I got to finish my degree at a prestigious university. Fucking a hot, arrogant man I'd loathed for years.

I couldn't control the quiver that caught my chest and the tightness of my muscles throughout me. His dizzying power continued to intensify, affecting me in new ways. "Yes — Master."

"Keep your head up." He released my hair and leaned further onto me. The long cock that pressed against the length of my slit terrified me, but not so much as I'd expected.

What added to the angst was when his weight on me lessened and the collar fitted around my neck. It didn't cause pain, but the ramifications were enough to terrify me, nonetheless. I'd already let him claim me, so he could do anything he wanted.

Despite the anxiety bubbling within me, the humiliation filled me with a rush of adrenaline. The sting that continued to buzz against my backside from the earlier spanking added to the physical pleasure of where his flesh pressed against mine. Every stroke of his length hit the perfect spot, building the absurd need within my foolish body to be fucked.

I expected him to put a condom on, but when his manhood pressed against my entry, I knew he had no intention of having safe sex with me.

"I have condoms," I said, pointing to my bedside table.

"Silence, slave." Another smack landed on my thigh. This one was more painful than the others.

I whimpered, but didn't dare argue against him. Did he know I was on birth control already, or did he simply not care whether he knocked me up?

The tension on the collar lessened, and the slight pain from it intensified my desire. When he dropped onto his elbows to either side of my head, and his body rested against my back in his effort to thrust, he had me pressed to the mattress. His girth didn't immediately enter me with the forceful motion.

My boyfriend's significantly smaller penis did me no favors when it came to sex with a new partner. With a man like this ready to force his cock into my drenched cunt, I'd needed something bigger to prepare me.

"I haven't fucked a pussy this tight in my life." He pulled back before shoving again, cock penetrating a little more, already beginning to fill me but continuing.

I bit back a pained cry as he finally thrust deep and hard. The pleasurous pain added to the awareness of knowing he had all the control over how rough or gentle this would be.

"A real cock feels good, doesn't it, little slave?"

Keep him happy. I had to turn my face to the side to speak. "Yes—Master."

He reared back, then shoved in, deep and owning of every inch inside me. I'd thought I wanted him to hurry and get this over with so I could see my boyfriend. Now I didn't think I could hide this adulterous act. This dominating male knew how to own a woman's body in a way that would leave his mark.

Once his speed increased, he raised upright and gripped my waist with both hands, pulling me backwards a little. Every thrust had him pounding in a way that brought an uncontrollable moan to my lips. I'd seen this kind of rough and fast fucking in porn, but I'd never thought I would receive it.

Chapter Three: Obey Me

My hands dug into the bedding, though it didn't actually provide any stability. The yank to the collar wrapped around my neck did hold me in place, though. Now I realized everything I'd been missing with my five-minute, missionary-only boyfriend.

This man, who didn't bother to remind me of his name, had no desire to keep things boring. His incessant angling hit the perfect spot that brought me to a bliss I only ever experienced while alone with my vibrator. And I always preferred that to any man's touch. If not for the arrogant prick causing the physical reaction, I would make the act a recurrence.

That thought of how amazing he was at fucking became more true when he stopped and flipped me over, making me feel the emptiness without him inside me. I needed more. My legs spread wide, bidding him to enter me. The way he towered over me as he positioned between my thighs made him look like the fearsome Master he demanded me to call him.

"You don't cum until I give you permission." Even now, his dominant stare locked on me, daring me to do something to receive punishment. His hand turned, coiling the cord attached to the collar around his fist. "Understand, slave?"

The lingering sting to my backside still buzzed, and I had no desire to be punished further. "Yes." I tensed as his manhood slammed hilt deep into me. Had he not grabbed my hip, his hard thrust would have sent me further onto the bed.

"Yes, what?" The words were spoken through his clenched teeth.

"Master," I breathed, followed by a gasp. Had that hurt or felt good? Maybe a bit of both. At least it was delighting enough, I didn't want it to stop.

Instead of continuing to pump into me, he held in place, the tip of his cock all the way against my cervix. "Don't forget what I am to you again!"

He reached down to circle his thumb over my nub, slow and light but dangerously pleasing enough to bring me release. I loved and hated the sensation, the need for climax, but fear of punishment. He would bring me to a shameful bliss so he had the right to respond to the disobedience.

Dark eyes scanned my parted lips and worried brow, both of which gave away my inability to hold out much longer. Even the arch of my back must have delighted him in how his featherlight touch held so much control over me.

Then the gratification I'd attempted to refuse myself came in full force. What would happen? How would he react to my response to him?

When my hips convulsed, he pulled back and slammed into my contracting walls. This time, he also lost control over his ability to delay the inevitable. The depth he held himself brought a whimper to my lips, yet delighted me at the same time.

"You're in trouble now, little slave." He freed himself from inside me and took a few steps backward, pulling the leash, so I sat up. "Clean me," he snapped.

I had no clue what that meant, but I assumed he needed a shower. When I attempted to rise, he pulled downward on the cord, tugging my collar. This would prove annoying if he planned to keep me on this leash.

"With your mouth." He enunciated every word as he continued to pull low enough I had to bend downward.

I lowered onto my knees in front of him, casting a questioning glance upward. The act repulsed me. His demand excited me, and the danger of punishment motivated me to do exactly as he ordered.

As an obedient human pet on a leash, I gripped his still-firm cock and leaned forward to lick the tip. Hopefully that would suffice, because I had no intent of faking a delightful wag of my rear at the *privilege*.

His palm to the back of my head corrected my wish not to taste myself on him. "You'll learn to love it." He thrust into my mouth until my face made contact with his pelvis. The next moan had my fluttering gaze on his smug expression. "Good girl."

That satisfied response startled me. I hadn't experienced that kind of praise from anyone — ever. But this was a game to him, and I needed to accept that. Besides, praise meant he wouldn't be using pain as a punishment.

My tongue twirled and worked as I bobbed over the softening manhood. Stopping too soon meant pain, so I continued until the moment he pulled his cock from me.

"Hands behind your back and chest presented upward," he ordered, not even giving me time or freedom to adjust to a more comfortable position.

I obeyed, instantly uncertain as he studied my form and shook his head.

He reached down, cupping my chin and rubbing his thumb on my lower lip. "You have a lot to learn, little slave." He side-stepped past me and leaned over the bed, returning with the rope I'd seen upon my arrival in the room.

And just what did *learning a lot* mean? Was it for this one encounter? Or until I moved out, perhaps.

I swallowed, already filled with unease from his disappointment.

He returned to where he'd been in front of me. "Stand and turn around — not like that," he snapped as I leaned onto my palms to rise. "Hands remain behind you."

Though difficult to balance, I obeyed, stopping so close in front of him, his sweet breath rolled down my forehead. I licked my lips, choosing to look at the floor. The change in focus quickly turned to regret when his arm reared back, and the rope landed with a loud whack on my backside.

"Obey me," he commanded, and I did, spinning as quickly as possible. "Hands gripping above your elbows."

Again, this time without hesitation or question, I did as ordered. I had to hope he accepted me in this position; that he wasn't currently too disappointed. Instead of barking another order, I felt the rope beginning to wrap over a wrist, crisscrossing as he wrapped it around the connected forearm.

Once the rope wove my forearms and around my elbows, his fingertips roved down my right side, palm joining over the curve of my rear as he explored downward. Even if I wanted to fight the tickling sensation or the way the other hand joined in to spread both cheeks, I couldn't.

"The next time you disobey me, I'm going to own this as well." The touch went to my tight hole. "And I promise, little slave, I won't be gentle."

Chapter Four: Pretty Little Mouth

The man who demanded to be called Master inspected the ropes binding my arms behind my back. After holding a shoulder and pushing my mid back forward so my chest angled upward, he said, "That's better. Stay right there until I return." He connected the leash to the bed and left me there.

I'd assumed he'd return in about five minutes, maybe to punish me in some odd way. That didn't happen. Soon enough, the uncomfortable position had me slumping against the bed. Not that I got much freedom to move, given the shortness of the secured leash.

Maybe he wanted to give me time to question whether or not I could spend the next month enduring what he had planned for me. I could only conclude this would probably involve more than one encounter. This little act was worth the luxury apartment if only a few hours a week were required, and I could hide the shameful choice from my boyfriend.

I found a bit of joy from it when I received rare praise from him. Something about his occasional delight comforted me. No wonder he'd called me a slut. I'd shown an enjoyment of the degradation just like any slut.

As time ticked on, I started thinking about what would happen when my boyfriend came over. How would I explain the situation if he used his key to get in here and he found me like this? Tell him it was only temporary?

Claiming I had to pay my dues to this stranger wouldn't be seen positively. The discomfort probably made time feel faster than it actually was. If anything, the Master would come for another round, then release me and leave for a while, and I could call my boyfriend to tell him I'd meet him somewhere else.

At some point during the boring wait, I heard the distant knock on the door. The one I had feared occurring.

Shit!

Maybe my boyfriend wouldn't use his key, and he'd wait for me to call him. That was a stupid hope, most likely. We had a few classes together, so I didn't want to think about what he might say to other students about me. Things would end between us.

I breathed a little easier after about fifteen minutes passed and no one entered. I would need to let this Master know I didn't like wasting study time stuck like this. It might receive a reprimand, but I still had a life he needed to respect.

The plan didn't go over well when I heard the Master's voice past the door. "After the loss, she needs to take some of the semester off...yes..."

The doorknob clicked and turned.

My effort to twist sideways to block my boyfriend from seeing me naked and bound only made me look silly. He'd never seen me like this. We were comfortably vanilla in our sexual endeavors.

"Slave." The chiding voice followed the creak of the door. "You know that isn't how you were ordered to be."

Both men entered. My boyfriend held a small glass of an amber drink — most likely the whiskey he kept in constant supply here.

I responded to the man with a snap. "What the fuck, asshole?" I wouldn't hide my irritation with the mortifying humiliation.

My boyfriend waited in the doorway; a dazed, shocked expression on his face as he gobbled up the sight of me. More like forced it down. I doubted many people got off on a woman bound as I had been.

"I'm not dropping classes or tolerating humiliation!" My glower fell on the Master, whose wet locks fell forward on his brow. The prick even found the time to take a shower while he made me wait. Now I wondered if he'd known my schedule and planned this exact encounter.

He shut the door. "Sit," he ordered my boyfriend, who surprisingly obeyed and sat in the chair by the door. One might believe he submitted to orders more than me by how he'd not hesitated.

Directed to me, the Master's snarl held a warning that had my next swallow caught in my throat. "I've shown you more than enough leniency, slave."

The fear of what might come consumed me. My thigh still showed the scarlet glow of where his hand landed hard in punishment. Forget whether or not my boyfriend remained. The aftermath of my insubordination might leave me wishing I'd obeyed the order to wait and keep my mouth shut. But the repulsed response my boyfriend cast my way had me struggling between the emotions. Not that I loved him. We didn't even get along most of the time, but a breakup had never been a consideration on my part. He'd been the only man to have me before this rich prick decided I owed him something.

Repeated reminders flowed into my mind, though. I needed to finish college. Punishment — however terrifying or stinging it may be — ensured the rest of my life wouldn't be spent elderly-man-hopping like my mother chose to do. Though, the thought of this one man tormenting me brought another bout of throbbing between my legs.

He removed his shirt, tossing it to the floor in front of my boyfriend's feet. As the Master strode my way, he said, "I think it's time for you to get a small dose of the humiliation you're going to receive for your misdeeds."

No. My terrified expression couldn't morph to any more fear than it had. This position should have been enough to be deemed humiliating. Yet, the ache between my legs built at the thought.

"Not in front of my boyfriend..." actually soon to be ex. I shouldn't have said it. I shouldn't have spoken.

The man crouched once he stood in front of me, brows raised. Words spoken low — still in control. Always in control. "Now, now, little slave." He stroked my cheek with his thumb. "Are you asking to end our little arrangement for that small-dicked prick?"

God no. It was already over with my boyfriend. Even before the thought could complete in my mind, my head shook frantically.

Embarrassment in exchange for a future worth living respectably. At least good sex was involved.

The fingers at my cheek combed through my hair, before firmly clasping at my crown, still gentle, but in control of my movement. With his other hand, he reached over to free the leash that kept me kneeling. "You don't have a boyfriend."

And I knew I didn't have a boyfriend any longer. This Master already claimed I would never fuck anyone else while with him. Or, actually, *ever*, though I knew that to be an exaggeration.

"No boyfriend," I whispered. "Master."

"And by the time I'm done punishing you, you won't forget it. Will you, little slave?"

"No," I grudgingly replied. But I had to tack on "Master" for fear of the penalties and more shame in front of my now-ex.

"I'm going to be nice and help you keep that pretty little mouth quiet, so you don't say anything else foolish before knowing the consequences of your actions." He scrutinized every inch of me before freeing my hair and leaning forward to grab something else. He returned and swiftly shoved a ball past my lips and between my teeth, before cinching an attached strap around my head, holding it tight in my mouth.

My ex-boyfriend could see me. My mouth stretched around the ball uncomfortably, makeup smeared from the tears that had followed the painful swats, nude and exposed with reddened folds, and an even redder backside he'd probably see soon enough.

Chapter Five: Punishment Deserved

"**I** want you bent over this bed and ready to accept the punishment you deserve for your ill-behavior," the Master said. "And the only time you get to look at him is once you earn the right to ride my dick, so you can show him the real pleasure only I can give you. Understood?"

Why the fuck would my boyfriend even stay to see this? Had he been threatened as well? Maybe he would receive compensation. Or maybe he chose not to leave, because he would get off on watching another man humiliate me.

"Yes, Master." I obeyed the Master's order and rose, shamefully casting my eyes downward, slightly struggling as I moved, given the way my arms remained bound behind my back. He didn't provide me with a bit of help; only watched with likely disapproval.

I bent over the bed, swollen and reddened folds visible to my ex-boyfriend.

The Master kicked my feet apart, revealing even more of me. Would he find a way to humiliate me every time I offended him? I already knew ridicule would come when I got to class and sat next to my ex.

Something warm and wet pressed against my tight hole, causing me to squirm forward.

"I already warned you what would happen when you misbehaved." He pushed my back, so I lay on the mattress while he continued to push inside until finally stopping. "That should get your virgin ass ready for the fucking you will receive in front of *him*." He spoke the word of my ex with absolute revulsion.

Were he not in charge of my pain, I might have had a snarky response. Such foolishness wouldn't escape me now, though.

His splayed hand went to my backside, circling as though he planned to find the perfect spot to spank before pulling it away. The area no longer hurt, but I knew it was about to. This powerful man drew out the terror, causing me to tighten every muscle in fear of the pain. Not to mention the embarrassment of the plug in my tight rear hole. Would he really —

Pain. Agony like sitting on metal that had baked in the hot sun radiated through me. The ball in my mouth hindered the scream that escaped me. This was nothing like the sting earlier. Had he even used his hand? He must have, because it remained in place, massaging the spot.

The next time it no longer pushed against me, I made my attempt to wiggle away, but his other palm held firm to my lower back beneath my bound arms. The tears that blurred my vision permitted me to see nothing.

Another painful smack landed on the other side. This one may have been less hard, or maybe so much sting still held from the previous spanking, that I couldn't notice how hard it crashed against me. It still hurt bad enough for me to cry into the gag, though. Maybe he'd placed it there so I couldn't curse him. Possibly, he didn't want me to have the chance to beg him to stop.

He knocked my legs wider apart, and the next blow encompassed my already-aching core as well. That had me jolting forward. After three more, my throat ached from the unheard cries. And my jaw hurt even worse from the struggle to cry and the inability to relax my mouth.

"That was for not being in position." His fingers began to stroke the length of my very pained folds. "I may need to wait to dole out the spankings for the ten other unacceptable behaviors." His digits dipped into my slickened slit. Despite every throb and the sting, that touch felt indescribably magnificent in a way it shouldn't have. "Now then, how about you receive a portion of your punishment for calling me an asshole?"

I already lay the entirety of my weight on the bed. Hopefully, his next painful act wouldn't involve any effort from me.

He lowered beside me, wiping tear-soaked hair from my face before he continued the delightful strokes over my slit. "Look at me."

I obeyed, giving him my full, though blurry, attention.

"You've been a good girl for this." His praise made me want to cry, but I couldn't reason as to why. My eyes did sting even more with a pool of tears. "You know there's a lot more punishment to come, right?"

I nodded, my cheek rubbing against my comforter.

"I'm willing to reduce the punishment significantly, but only if you sit on my lap facing that low-life prick so he can watch you cum while my cock is in your ass."

Letting my folds and ass be seen was far different from seeing my facial expressions while being fucked. This choice seemed like the worst punishment so far. And there would be no way I could cum with that giant shaft in my rear hole. But to endure the humiliation, that seemed impossible.

If only I could speak, I'd want to know what he meant by significantly reducing the punishment.

"He's cheating on you, you know," the Master said. "And he has been for quite a while with a slutty little blonde sorority girl."

Now the humiliation stemmed from what I should have known about, but I thought that had only been a drunken mistake on his part. Yet he continued to hook up with her.

Every part of me ached, made worse by the way I bit the gag. Realistically, this relationship with my ex-boyfriend was doomed to end at the moment I'd let the wealthy heir's cock enter my mouth, but to know my ex spent his free time with another woman had every negative emotion imaginable building.

"What do you say, little slave?" The Master leaned forward, planting a kiss to my cheek. Kindly, maybe comforting me through the horror. "Don't you want him to see what I do to you?" he whispered.

Something about the affectionate way he spoke and the oddly comforting kiss had my attention return to him. At least he put on a good show to piss off the cheater who sat by the door. Given things had already gone so far, and my anger at my ex, I had no choice but to agree. Even with the shame of being seen this way, something magnetic had me wanting to please this self-proclaimed master of my being. And to let the liar watching us see me willingly fuck another man with a profoundly larger cock.

Chapter Six: Work For It

No matter the pain I knew would come, I could only reply to the Master with one answer — a nod of my head. I would make sure to enjoy this to some degree.

"I thought so, sweet girl." He gently reached to the thick plug and guided it out, tossing it toward my ex. What the fuck was wrong with him anyway for still watching us? I'd probably question that while remembering this moment for the rest of my life.

After the man sat on the edge of the bed, I rolled over toward him. This time, he did help me. I appreciated the show of care the Master performed, even if the concern for me would end when we were alone again. For now, his strong arm wrapped around my torso and lifted me while I faced toward my ex, who held the emptied whiskey glass in his hand, expression even more shocked.

The prick deserved this. He was a bossy and degrading cheater. A selfish in day and in bed asshole. I'd never even considered that until this moment.

This Master may have been dominating. He may have even been humiliating me, but he was the better choice until I received my diploma. He didn't force anything upon me. Despite the torment I still felt at my rear and slit, he'd done nothing but make me feel good in his conquest to have me. The means at which he had me willing to be his toy may have been questionable, but I couldn't care less, so long as it pissed off the bastard across the room.

There I was, raised in the Master's strong arms, face directed toward my ex. I didn't want to look at him. Every memory of the ways he'd treated me came roaring back. Things I never thought of at the time we were together. The insults, the silent judgments, the other woman, the way I was never good enough. No spanking or rough fucking hurt as much as knowing what I'd once settled for.

If I weren't gagged, I'd tell him to go fuck himself. He wasn't worth an ounce of my concern.

Even now, the spot where the man kissed my cheek buzzed with excitement. I couldn't forget the predicament I'd caused myself to be in, though.

His shaft pressed against my pre-stretched and lubed back hole. This would happen, and it would be punishing for my outburst for a man I shouldn't have given a fuck about. At the discomfort, my eyes squeezed shut. Even worse, he knocked my thighs apart and lowered my still burning rear all the way onto him.

"That's it, slave," he moaned. "You want forgiveness for insulting me, don't you?"

I nodded with vigor. Yes, to forgiveness and pleasing him, even if it hurt, and his gargantuan cock had its way with my hole.

His arms were tight around me, able to lift and lower me. Even when he switched to one arm curled over me, he was able to continue, adding the rock of his pelvis. His freed hand reached up to uncinch the gag.

When it fell, I took a much-needed deep breath. I still wanted to keep my lips tight. I didn't want a single whimper or moan to escape.

He let that palm rove down to my breast, cupping and squeezing. His breath tickled my left shoulder, bringing a shiver to my chest. "Thank me for making you feel good," he ordered.

"Thank you, Master," I replied, the word ending on a gasp as he slammed painfully upward into me.

His hand went down to my slit, stroking the sensitive nerves that silently begged and thrummed for his touch. The moan he elicited caught me off guard, as though I couldn't believe such a sound of bliss could come from me.

I wanted to hold back and not let my ex see my response or hear the uncontrollable moans and gasps. I bit my lower lip.

"I didn't remove that gag so you would be silent." He rammed upward, bringing a whimper before his fingers furiously clamped and worked against that bundle of nerves that loved every moment. "I'm going to hear your pleasure or your pain, little one."

I freed the building groan, spreading my legs wider for him. His fucking would feel so much better as soon as my mind wasn't haunted by my ex's cheating. I could rush an orgasm if it meant he left my life. If only the Master didn't slow that pleasuring tease to the sensitive spot, switching to rocking his cock into me, humming his own approval against the back of my neck. Then the pressure went to my nub again, but this time, he held still.

"Work for it, slave," he demanded, sliding fingers into me as the heel of his palm demanded I thrust against it. "And I want that prick to hear the pleasure only I can provide you with."

My hips rolled as he continued his in-and-out of me. Even my existing presence wouldn't hinder me from this journey to climax. It didn't take long before my walls were tightening on his fingers, and I moaned my pleasure.

That was only the beginning of the endeavor. Once I had mine, his strong arms crisscrossed over my chest so he could palm my breasts and steer my body along his length faster and harder. Painful and exciting, shameful while exhilarating.

The thought of how much this must have upset my ex gave me some relief. At any other point, or under different circumstances, a break-up would have been hard. This man didn't plan to let me dwell on it. He wanted me to feel every inch as he pumped into me. No other man mattered anymore.

He climaxed with a strong explosion of seed pulsing into me, humming his approval along my shoulder blades. His grip remained firm as he growled. "Now get the fuck out and stay away from her unless you want to see how quickly I can ruin your life!"

My ex hadn't seemed unwilling to see me upon arrival, but that suggested there was more to their discussion than I got to hear. I never saw my ex bolt from a room so quickly, but I loved seeing his unease. But the moment he left, I knew exactly what he would be doing. By tomorrow, most of the people we knew would have caught all the details of what he witnessed me doing with a man I'd only met hours ago.

"And you, little slave," the Master said, unbudging. "I'm nowhere near done punishing you."

Chapter Seven: Inappropriate Relations

The self-proclaimed Master made me crawl on hands and knees beside him. He had the leash so tight, if I didn't stay right at his side, it would pull the collar. If the collar jerked at all, a riding crop would land on my still-stinging backside.

After a loop around my room and then into the main area of my apartment, the man asked, "Have any men you had inappropriate relations with sat on that couch?"

What kind of dumb question was he asking? "Inappropriate relations?" I repeated, both snarky and innocent.

Instead of bothering with the crop, he leaned down and smacked my rear, reigniting the sting from previous punishment. "Look at me when I speak to you."

Startled by his aggressive reaction, I obeyed.

"Sit correctly." He raised the crop to my shoulder, pressing, so I lowered until my rear rested on my ankles. "That's my good girl." The affectionate shift in his tone and the gentler expression could make anyone forget the torment he'd inflicted moments earlier. "I don't want our first day together doing nothing but punishing you, so look at me when we speak, answer my questions respectfully, and don't forget to address me properly."

"Yes, Master."

He assessed all of me as I waited for his next demand.

"Did *he* ever sit on any of the furniture?" he asked.

I looked at the blue leather couch, but the flap of the crop tapped my chin to guide my face in his direction. "Yes, Master."

"Is there any other furniture he touched?"

My ex had exhibited jealousy, but not to the extent of concerning himself with furniture. This seemed absurd.

"All of it," I replied, adding, "Master."

"That would be a *yes, Master*." He scanned the area with disgust. The long exhale that followed didn't quite seem to be a sigh, but I had to assume some annoyance. "You've already stolen more than a hundred thousand dollars of my inheritance, and replacing all this tainted furniture will probably cost you at least another twenty-K."

My brow furrowed. I'd stolen nothing.

This tolerance of the cocky man that I would endure had to do with having a place to live until I finished university. In some ways, he was intriguing, but in others, I found him pompous. The finances had to be an exaggeration on his part. I wouldn't be able to work off a hundred and twenty thousand dollars. I wasn't going to willfully subject myself to another spanking, though.

"Yes, Master." It was the only thing I knew to say without argument.

He tapped a finger on his chin as he stared down to my breasts. It wasn't a long interest in my nude form. "Until the soiled furniture is replaced, you remain on the floor. Not that you're well behaved enough to deserve a chair to sit on, anyway." He smiled down at me. "Speaking of, I think my little slave is hungry."

Was I? I hadn't eaten all day to ensure I could fit in the form-fitting dress I'd planned to wear with my ex. Going a little longer without a meal wouldn't bother me at all. But for a little over a month to go, I could gain a few pounds if necessary.

"Let's go," he commanded. "I need to let you clean up, and then I'll order food."

Take away the coercion, and he seemed like a charming man. The smile and smooth skin, the way that clump of hair fell forward. Mostly, though, the intensity of his magnetic stare.

From across a room he could turn heads, and yet he looked down to me with passion. Like he genuinely wanted me. A look that would have me singled out and blushing in the most crowded place. The same look flashed my way as he had at his father's funeral. It was brief then, hostile in my assumption. Maybe it was the moment he first considered coming to my apartment to demand I gratify him.

I should have been repulsed by his assumption, but, at my core, I must have craved the same things my mother sought in a man. And now I knew she didn't only fake her way with wealthy men, she genuinely enjoyed them. More than the money and attractiveness people saw on first glance, but the primal domination radiating. But I wouldn't permit the craving to rule over my life as she did.

I licked my lower lip; a behavior he noticed.

One side of his mouth raised, but not in a grin. Smug, as though he'd already broken me. "Come along, slave." He turned and waited for me to move into position beside him.

Another uncomfortable crawl led me straight to my bathroom, where he turned on the shower. "Wait and keep your eyes on me," he commanded.

I lowered my backside to my ankles in the position he expected. This submission came far too quickly, as though it had been missing from my life and I'd been starved of a necessity.

He cleansed himself off first, not bothering to look at me until he'd finished washing his hair. It was then I became aware he'd brought his own soaps and shampoo. This had never been a simple visit.

Chapter Eight: A Valuable Lesson

He soon ordered me into the shower, saying, "Stand and come in front of me."

As I had done since his arrival, I continued to follow his orders. Some had to do with fear of repercussions, but most had to do with the softer side that praised me and the smoldering glances. I could probably blame it on what my ex had done. At this point in my crashing world, kindness felt like the only comfort.

Once I stood in front of him in the spray of the warm water, he washed my hair, slowly massaging my scalp. I hadn't known what to expect of a shower with a man, but he made it comforting. Romantic. I couldn't say I'd ever experienced this sort of touch. True, I needed the shower, but it felt different from how I believed he would behave.

He collected the soap and lathered it in his hands before a smooth glide along my arms. "If you continue to be this good, I might let you sit on my lap while you eat."

As he caressed my breasts, I considered telling him I didn't need to sit on his lap like a child, but my knees and rear had enough abuse that I didn't want to eat dinner on them.

"Would you like that, slave?" He may have been irritated by my lack of answer or the possible annoyance in my expression.

"Yes," I replied, "Master."

His hand meandered down between my legs. I wasn't certain whether he cared more about cleaning the sex from my nether regions or watching my response to the way he stroked me. "You're being so very good for me, slave." He stepped close so our wet bodies touched.

When his face lowered, I didn't expect his intent was to kiss me. Yet the soft connection of our lips felt natural. *He* felt natural.

"It's nice being good, isn't it, slave?" His mouth remained close to mine, my every breath swelling toward him, so his body grazed my nipples that tingled in response.

"Yes, Master."

"I'm going to need to be creative with your punishment so I can enjoy it as much as the rewards you would have received otherwise." Now he kissed me again, but this time more firmly. "And I love being creative. Especially considering your behaviors toward me all these years."

I swallowed, wondering whether the offense he claimed was genuine or an act. He'd been the jerk, not me. I never remained in his presence to behave in any way toward him. "We could start over."

"I didn't give you permission to speak," he said, gripping me by my wet hair. The hold didn't hurt, but it held a warning. That expectation of me only mattered until the middle of December, when my classes ended and I graduated. Short enough that this would remain engaging for him, and not insufferably long for me.

Once we finished the shower, he dried me off and commanded me to my hands and knees. I wasn't permitted to do anything but look at him as he ordered food delivery and then awaited its arrival in the foyer. He probably knew my intolerance of fish, so that was what he ordered.

True to his word, after he had the meal set out, he sat with his side to the table and let me sit on his lap, facing it. The only noise for the meal was my fork scraping the plate. He made eating a challenge with his slow and seemingly unaware strokes of his knuckles over my breast. The peaks were equally aroused and responsive to how cold my nude body felt.

Soon enough, he chuckled, causing me to stop to see why I'd humored him. He'd already tapped the table every time I put the fork down. I was to eat every bite, no matter how long it took.

He beamed and kissed my shoulder. "I still remember the day I met your mother."

I swallowed; a bit bothered by hearing about her as he toyed with my left breast.

"My father had invited his business partner and a few investors over." He laughed again and shook his head. "That was the day she learned a valuable lesson about his expectations of her." He pulled my hip, so I faced him a bit more. "Ask me why," he ordered.

"Why...Master?"

"She didn't have dinner prepared on time, so we all had to wait fifteen extra minutes. Then she went to sit by my father as though she'd done nothing wrong." He ran his palm along my thigh. "Before she landed in her chair, he had her yanked onto his lap and lifted her skirt." That same roving hand went between my legs to my slit, slightly dipping his fingers into the moisture his ongoing fondling had caused.

"He spanked her until her ass was red as a rose before bending her onto the table." His following smile was no less than villainous. "I still remember her whimpers from his body slapping against the sensitive area. Oh, but after he filled her with seed, he flipped her over."

His fingers dipped into me, sending my overly sensitive core into want that would only cause a painful pleasure.

"He then belted her pussy until his dick was ready again." He spoke far too fond of the memory. "Thank God you don't have ridiculous fake tits like hers." The Master whose manner began to worry me leaned forward to lick the nipple he'd been toying with all of dinner.

He hummed against my breast before returning upright. "God, the way they jiggled but maintained their fake form had the CFO on the table with electro clamps latched to her tits that made her mewl even louder."

I'd grown sick of this story. I didn't want to hear about men doing things to my mother or how her tits looked. Certainly, I didn't care to learn she pleasured his father and his business associates. My attempt to face the wall ahead was met with his hand to my jaw, forcing my focus onto him.

"He used the silver chains that were attached to the nipple clamps like they were reins while she tilted her head back so she could suck his dick. She needed a few zaps to remind her of how to suck and fuck like a good slave that was too old to be bred by one owner."

I had no doubt my horror showed. They treated her that way because of her age? And she endured it over hopes for a portion of the old man's money? More than ever, I knew choosing her lifestyle would lead to self-destruction.

I feared this story. This man could punish me however he wanted. His father had been a donor to the elite university. One order could have professors unwilling to pass me. He could have me tossed onto the street. I would lose everything if I pissed him off. Yet right now, he leaned against me with a lover's care. But it was just part of a month-long game that would at least help me forget about my ex. I had to rationalize my agreeableness somehow.

Now he beamed more than I'd seen in the entire half day we'd been together. "You have no idea how much I'm looking forward to continuing your punishment for every single bad thing you've done, little slave."

Chapter Nine: Wait

To make the day spiral worse, the Master followed our early dinner by walking me through the apartment. For close to an hour, he snooped through my belongings.

By the time he was done, he had a pile of all my undergarments, lingerie, any pictures of my ex, and any gifts I'd received from him. Not that there were many presents I'd received. He also added in any jewelry that I had, aside from a ring my mom gifted me.

When I got the courage to argue, he'd spanked me and threatened to gag me and fuck me again in my tight hole. I didn't so much as peep an objection after that.

One month.

I was back to being ready to be rid of him. So far, he'd coerced me, spanked me, fucked me, humiliated me, and fucked and spanked me even more. But something about the charming side of him pulled me back in. The hint of praise, a two second caress, the enchanting gaze. Somehow those micro moments were more memorable than the punishment and humiliation.

After he studied the trash pile of anything I'd ever worn for another man, he slumped down on the elegant armchair no one ever used, except for leaving purses and belongings. The only furniture I could keep, since I'd later clarified that no one ever tarnished it.

I had to wonder if this Master would be as jealous as my cheating ex. We weren't a couple, so jealousy seemed ridiculous.

"Kneel here, facing me, slave." He pointed to the floor in front of him.

I crawled over to wait on my knees below his harsh scowl. The black leather strip on the end of his crop tickled down to my right nipple, flooding me with bizarre excitement at the sensation.

The punishment device reared backward and slapped my chest before I knew it was even coming. "Arch your back properly and place your hands on your thighs."

I obeyed, fighting the whimper that wanted to escape as I angled my breasts upward for his viewing pleasure. Not that I got a bad view of his toned body in nothing more than the black satin boxers he wore. He had the body type of a man who could turn heads in passing. Both sexy and a dominating jerk whose orders returned to being any way he could humiliate me.

A knock on the door startled me. The only person who ever came here at night was my ex-boyfriend. Hopefully, he hadn't come back to lash out at me and hadn't told any of my friends to see what was happening.

The crop tapped the bottom of my chin, directing my eyes to the Master's. Or, perhaps, him permitting me to look at his overly handsome features. "You only look at me in the presence of others, and you remain in position."

"Yes, Master," I replied, already concerned about who would see me naked and kneeling. Maybe he'd found a professor of mine to top the shame after the last viewer.

But a tingle stirred in my core at the thought of being the man's personal fuck-toy again. To be seen as his in the most violating way. And punished if I dared to misbehave or act in a way that suggested displeasure.

"Enter," he called, before the door opened and steps could be heard. More than one set.

"I need to direct them on everything to be rid of and where to place my new furniture. Wait here with eyes to the floor. Understood?"

My gaze lowered. "Yes, Master."

"That's my good girl." His compliment caused me to look up, quickly receiving a painful swat of the crop to my left breast and another to the right. "That," he growled, "was not good. Until I say otherwise—Eyes. To. Floor!"

I felt the shame of the reprimand, knowing anyone working in my apartment heard it. And they certainly saw me in this humiliating position.

"If you misbehave again, I'll have the movers take a break and watch me teach you a lesson in a similar way to how your mom had to be taught."

This threat would be worse than the embarrassment in front of my ex—far, far worse. At least resentment fueled my ability to enjoy some of the things happening when the cheater watched.

"Understood," I replied, words directed toward his bare feet. "Master."

This time, I didn't move, nor did I dare attempt to see what went on in my periphery. Even when men stepped within a foot from my side, I didn't budge to shield my upward breasts from view.

Too much time passed, and even with that threat lingering, no one could sit with such an arch to their back and straightened shoulders for hours. Certainly not me. My muscles and knees began to ache, but to move meant any number of possible punishments. Though they could also have been exaggerated threats from a man who'd known how to horrify and charm me.

Eventually, without a sound of him nearby, I let my shoulders relax, taking in that deep breath of relief. But the moment steps returned, I got in position too quick to be caught.

The movement all around subsided when strong hands began to knead my sore shoulders. This had been an excessively long and torturous day, so I would accept one of his shows of mock affection.

"I was hoping to give you a long massage and a lavender bath, slave." One of those firm hands went to my throat. Fingers pressed to the area beneath my chin, forcing my face upward to his. "But you disobeyed me again and thought you would still be rewarded." He leaned down to hiss against my ear. "They're still putting the bed together, but I can make use of what is already set up in my room."

His room. I could only imagine what kind of bedroom a man like him would have. I feared to know for certain, though. I still had welts and aches, so the last thing I wanted was him using professional grade domination equipment on me.

Trepidation filled me the moment he ordered me to crawl at his side; worsening as we neared the bedroom. Terrifying me when I looked up to the three men putting together metal pieces that appeared like they fit together to be a cage.

A thick black rail already crossed the ceiling, with hooks protruding every few feet. *Hooks? Seriously.* Like he planned to somehow use those with me?

My palms dug into the carpet, but then the crop landed hard on my rear, causing me to yelp.

"Don't make this worse than it has to be," he snapped, "disobedient little slave!"

Chapter Ten: A Slight Improvement

I panicked at the sight of the three very buff men who looked in my direction. The newest humiliation involved being fucked in their presence in a room with a partial cage and hooks hanging down from the ceiling for a *who-knows-what* kind of sick fetish. This bordered on being too much for me to maintain my sanity and willingness to remain agreeable with the arrogant man who deemed himself my master.

But what choice would there be? After hearing the story of my mom, I didn't dare risk anything going wrong with my education.

One month. One month. One fucking month!

"Kneel," he ordered, pointing in front of him.

I circled around to assume the position he'd commanded me to, presenting my breasts for him to view.

"A slight improvement," he said. "Maybe you don't need the lesson your mother had to learn from." The soft flap of the riding crop tapped my nub in a way that gave enough stimulation to bring my body to react with craving. He continued, "I don't think these men have ever seen a woman tortured into a climax."

Tortured! Tortured? What did that even mean? I wasn't too eager to find out, given the torrent in his gaze. He wouldn't cross boundaries into serious harm. At least, I didn't think so.

But then again, I didn't know him well enough to know for certain. His father had been a powerful man people knew not to offend. The geriatric millionaire apparently did mean things to my mother — but things she enjoyed.

The flap continued to caress the area, teasing with the opportunity to show my pleasure, and the humiliation of my response being seen by a leering crew of men that I never wanted to let see me unclothed. I hadn't even gotten a long look at them yet, but I didn't need to.

"Let me hear you moan, slave." The crop stroked my nub again with a friction that received a minute bump of my hips to feel it a little longer.

I batted my pleading eyes upward, wanting him to order the men out, but he didn't.

"Gentlemen, feel free to take a break and enjoy my little slave's love of being watched as I use her and she cums hard." He wiped a lock of hair from my brow. "I'm going to need for you to hold your wrists out in front of you so I can bind them."

At least my hands wouldn't be bound behind my back as they had been earlier.

I extended them in front of me to his expectant hand. The thing I didn't like about being tied up was how helpless I'd been. I could do nothing to protect myself, and I remained at his mercy with restraints.

"Please," I whispered, connecting our gaze. I added, "Master."

He crouched in front of me. "You disobeyed me, little slave." He began to wrap a cord of rope around my wrists.

His long, slow sigh that followed suggested second thoughts. Maybe he would find another way to punish me.

"You will learn nothing from your ill behavior if I give in to pouts or tears. No more begging, or I will ask them to assist me in your punishment."

At that cruel threat, I nodded my understanding. Now I really understood why he shared the story about my mom. Not that I needed to know it in order to behave.

University fees, a place to live, amazing sex without thoughts of my cheating ex. One month. A little humiliation was worth all of that. Once the men were gone, I would never think about them again.

After he'd woven the soft white rope with a loop extending from it, he rose, carefully guiding me up as well. His kind helpfulness through the act made this worse. He couldn't be accused of being a psychotic asshole. Right now, he was just a nice, calm man needing to punish my ill actions — publicly.

While raising my hands over my head, he flashed a grin that would have been handsome under normal circumstances. Given the situation, I could only assume it would be a grin of delight in whatever shameful thing he planned to subject me to. Still, I didn't lose a bit of arousal through it all. My unbidden excitement increased as adrenaline pumped through me, and my heart raced.

"On your toes." He extended the loop of the rope to a hook above where I stood in the center of the room. "I need for you to turn around so these men get to watch your every reaction to my touch."

"Yes, Master," I replied, squinting my eyes shut as I turned on the balls of my feet. This would be another way of exhausting my muscles. People needed to work up to the strains I'd been enduring over the course of the day. Half of a day at most, yet they'd been the most eventful hours of my entire life.

"You're going to need to keep your eyes open, slave."

Of course he would require that.

"Consider this as preparation for how you will be disciplined for the attitude and ill behavior in front of that little prick," he said, hands gripping my waist and roving upward to cup my breasts. The hold and the way he circled the stiff peaks brought a delight I struggled to not express.

"You know," he purred behind me, pressing his body to mine, so I could feel his erection at my back. "A woman's response to a man's touch to her nipples is the same hormone released when she's falling in love." He rolled his fingers over the pebbled tips.

Yet again, he knew how to add a tormenting touch and tone that felt caring and comforting. His breath tickled over my neck. "Let these men see how much you already love me and want my punishment."

Chapter Eleven: Clamped

I did want his touch. He'd somehow made certain I wanted to feel him, but not in this shameful way. And we both knew this had nothing to do with love. Fighting a response seemed futile, though. Then again, the struggle within me made the sensation stronger. Touch to my nipples alone felt as though they would eventually set off my release.

He only spent a few minutes massaging my breasts, grinding his cock against me, and teasing my neck with kisses, but my core felt the desperation for a tiny bit more from him. For that touch. For the release that I didn't want these strangers to see.

"You're trying to hide your pleasure of my touch from these men, aren't you?" he asked.

"Yes," I admitted. I couldn't lie if I tried. "M–Master."

"Tsk, tsk, little slave," he replied, squeezing and pulling with his right hand, before letting it explore downward and stealing it away from my flesh. "I have just the thing for that."

When it returned, he squeezed the breast he held with his left hand and clamped something onto the nipple.

No, I'd rather do anything over what he'd enjoyed mentioning had been done to my mother. Would he let someone else be involved? A mover at that. I didn't want any of them touching me.

My whimper received no response from him. He gripped the other, placing another clip. With both painfully clamped, I quivered, struggling on my toes.

"If I think you're holding back, I will have to use these," he said sternly. A shock bolted into me from the clips he'd attached to my breasts. It felt like his boastful story about my mother, but she probably wanted the multiple men and pain.

I squeaked, fearful of another zap to come.

"Not quite high enough, is it?" The next shock sent a bolt into me that caused a jump. "That's better. Now then, I have a dildo that uses electro stimulation as well if I need." His voice went husky against my trembling shoulder. "Will my bad little slave be needing that as well? I only have so many hands to punish you with." A threat of the possibility of letting someone else be involved.

I panted, terrified of the pain and the possibility of strangers helping inflict it. "N — no." This had been a roller coaster, slightly bumpy at first, but suddenly too terrifying.

Another shock made me cry out.

"No, what?" The cruel jerk didn't even give me the additional moment to speak his title.

"Master!"

"Careful with the attitude. I'll be right back. I need to get a stool to get comfortable."

Someone chuckled.

With the introduction of torture, I'd actually pushed aside the presence of the three moving men whose heads I could look above. Such pain would do that to a person. And I wouldn't dare give them the glance that made them seem like real people in the room.

The scrape of something dragging along the floor preceded his return. His cock pressed to my lower back again, threatening to add another sort of punishment. *University and housing.* I snarled as the next thought came — *amazing sex.*

Like this torture was considered amazing? Not in the least. It was horrifying.

Or was it? There was still that blissful pleasure mixed with the pain of the clamps.

He lifted me, then scooted the stool closer before seating himself and resting me on his lap. My arms remained bound and connected up high. My breasts swayed with the Master's movements. Hopefully, he wouldn't decide to use the connections to the clamps as reins.

He spread my legs wide for the three men to see my bare slit. "Their mouths are watering at the sight and smell of your needy cunt, little slave. Can you see that?"

I nodded emphatically to let him know that I was aware of the desire of the men.

A painful zap overtook my breasts, causing me to buck forward, but caught by the bindings and his hands that seemed prepared to keep me steady.

"I don't think you actually made sure they were all watching."

"Master," I whimpered. Couldn't he get this over with? He must have been enjoying it too much.

His right hand went down to my slit as I gave each perverted moving man an individual assessment. All were somewhere in the range of late twenties to mid-thirties. None ugly, but they weren't the sort of men I'd ever cross paths with and talk to at the prestigious university.

"That's my good little slave. Now then, let them know how much you love my thumb stroking your clit." His cock ground at my backside as he placed pressure on my nub, flicking it with his attention to my every quiver.

I gasped, rocking my hips forward. A lesser shock went to my nipples, adding to the blissful feeling of his touch.

This had me moaning about my need; hushed, but not too controlled for fear of punishment.

"Oh, slave, you're turning me on." His husky voice filled me with more excitement. He zapped me again, finger dedicated to my nub in a furious vibration that had me biting my lip as the overwhelming stimulation continued. "I'm going to need for you to hold yourself up while I pull down my pants and then fuck you into oblivion."

Chapter Twelve: Setting Up

I wouldn't have argued against his orders anyway, but the Master believed I took too long to support my own weight. The powerful zap that radiated through my nipples forced a yelp from me — and he didn't seem concerned in the least at my pain. Not that I wasn't leaking with need and aching at my core for sexual release. He'd probably already caused a mental illness within me, even though he'd only had me for half of the day. I wouldn't accept any other reason for my responses to him.

Once I had a somewhat stable hold to pull myself up, and a spot on the stool to place a foot on for added support, I felt certain I'd been successful. Nothing proved that until he'd shuffled from his pants and positioned his cock at my entrance.

Another long zap ricocheted through me, causing me to cry out from the torment, and for him to groan his delight.

"I love the way you squeeze me when you feel that shock. I'm going to have to keep doing it until you make me cum, little slave."

Now he gave me a reason to rush this. Lowering myself, my trembling legs spread wider as I sought out the bars on the stool my feet could use as support. Another zap made me aware of the urgency. But what if I gave him pleasure but couldn't bring my own? Would I be punished?

Another bolt of current warned that I needed to begin. He needed his orgasm, so I struggled with my strange balance. I looked like a frog about to leap, and I had no doubt I delighted the movers when my breasts began to bounce as I rode the Master's long, ridged cock.

"Slave," he hummed, zapping my nipples with a powerful shock. "You feel so fucking amazing. Let me hear you moan your pleasure." His fingertips went between my legs again. Not only would I be in this silly position riding his shaft, but I'd be enjoying myself, and everyone would see that bliss on my face. I did moan as he rammed his cock upward into me and gripped my right hip, forcing me to work harder against his hold.

The zaps at my breasts came closer together, causing me to clamp down on his manhood each time. Bringing him to moan his own desires. Both of us soaring into bliss at the expense of my torment.

Even through the newfound pain he exposed me to, stronger desire burned. I wouldn't have ever thought such a shock could send my body on a collision course with gratification. But, before this man who claimed me as his slave, I wouldn't have believed an orgasm through intercourse was possible.

The Master fisted the hair at my nape and pulled back, turning my head, so I looked to him. "Want to cum, don't you, slave?"

I would have nodded, but his forceful grip didn't permit. "Yes," I moaned the word, barely remembering to add, "Master." I did want it. I wanted to feel him pulsing inside me. I wanted to explode.

Shocks radiated through me, bringing a sinister hum from him.

"I'm going to make you cum so hard." His hold to my hair pulled me so my lips connected to his, roughly kissing me as though my mouth needed to be claimed as much as my cunt needed his ownership.

My sore arms could hardly hold me up much longer. Not that they'd done much, but my legs that had been doing most of the work felt just as exhausted. He started pounding upward, relieving me to feel him within my walls as I held in place, trembling with burning muscles, but awakened within. The shocks didn't stop. They picked up, jolting me every few seconds and eliciting a gasp as I clenched against his manhood in response.

The pain and pleasure had me crying out with every thrust he claimed me with. My orgasm came first with my walls clamping down on his eager cock, followed by repeated shocks to my breasts and his harder pounding.

His ragged breath heated my sweaty back while fingertips dug into the soft flesh at my middle. This was rougher and more dominating than he'd been. This bordered me losing all ability to maintain hold. His final slam into me remained in place, pulsing into my spasming slit.

My weight gave out onto him, my arms pulled tight from where they were anchored to the ceiling. To say he knew how to please and torment my body would be an understatement. He owned my pleasure and torment. He let me experience sexuality in ways unimaginable before today.

He kissed my shoulder. "We still have a few hours of work setting my room up, so I'm going to need for you to stand here and wait for us."

"Master." My whimper attempted to relay my exhaustion and plea for mercy. I needed to clean up, not have a man's seed leaking from me in front of all these men.

"Bad slaves don't get requests." He didn't give me the opportunity to ask to be clean. This would still be punishment for my inability to maintain position earlier. A few more hours, aching, struggling on the tips of my toes, exposed to these extremely aroused men. Torture, just as he'd mentioned.

Chapter Thirteen: Self-control

The new king-sized bed included a cage beneath it with vertical bars, like a jail cell. I still squirmed in the horrid position he'd left me standing in. After the movers left, and he'd lay sheets on the bed, he plopped down on it, watching me.

I probably looked like a pathetic mess while attempting to stand on the tips of my toes to spare my arms from the strain of where they were bound to a hook. He seemed to relish the disturbing sight.

"I hope you like my new furniture," he said, beaming with self-satisfaction. "Assuming I let you remain in college—" he patted the mattress "—there's a nice place for you to study and call your own home just beneath my bed."

I hid my desire to snarl or whimper. Of course, he wouldn't refuse me classes. That was the only reason he had this power over me. But if I were to make a peep and point that out, he'd punish me longer.

I didn't want anything further done to me. I just wanted to bathe and sleep. And stupidly, I wanted him beside me. I needed someone close after this tormenting day.

After he'd had his fun taunting me, he finally came to stand in front of me, plunging a finger between my folds before trailing the soaked digit up my tummy all the way until it reached my mouth where he pushed it in.

"That's the only cum you're ever going to get from now on, slave." His hot and cold behaviors proved both intriguing and frustrating. Right now, not something I cared for.

I was exhausted but pointing that out might only give him more craving to torment me, so I decided to continue feeding his desire to be my Master. "I only want your cum, Master."

"Good girl," he cooed, contented with my response. He reached up to remove the binding on my wrists from where it connected to the hook. "You were bad today, so you need to go straight to sleep."

"Can I have a shower, Master?" I asked as I lowered my still-bound hands in front of me.

"Are you saying you have a problem with my cum?"

"No, Master," I mumbled.

"I'll bathe you in the morning. For now —" he went to the end of the bed and opened the cage door. "I want you to brush your teeth and use the bathroom, then crawl in here and go to sleep."

I could only stare at the lower area beneath the mattress in horror. Crawl down there and sleep? That seemed like a joke, but his expectant tap of his foot at the entry suggested this was very real.

A diploma and housing. Could I play along to ensure graduation? It seemed near unlikely I could tolerate his ridiculous expectations if they continued with this extremeness.

In the end, I obeyed, spending a long cold and miserable night naked on a thin mat. Why was he toying with me? He'd come in and shaken my world, and he'd arrived prepared with plenty of ammo to make sure I surrendered.

After my thoughts finally slowed, it felt like I'd only drifted to sleep for a few minutes when he woke me with a loud call. "Slave!"

We'd stayed up way too late, and the sun hadn't even risen yet. Beyond that, I never woke before late morning.

He wouldn't give me that luxury. Not when he ridiculously expected me to earn every penny his father spent on me.

The moment I rolled, the agony of worn muscles took hold. Moving hurt. I wasn't lazy by any means, but he'd forced too much upon my muscles. I doubted he intended to let them recover, either. I slowly crawled out to where he stood in wait. Behind him, soft lighting from the bathroom gave my room a small bit of illumination.

When I attempted to stand, a heavy hand blocked my shoulder.

"Crawl to the bath and get in."

"Seriously?" I grumbled, but accepted he wouldn't allow me to stand upright. It was a bit agitating that this was still going on. "You had a fun day of tormenting me, but I won't crawl around all the time."

A zap landed on my shoulder from a stick he placed against it. It looked like a magic wand, except it was designed for shocking. I winced, but before I could say anything else, he spoke.

"I hoped our day could start pleasant, but if this is how you plan to act, then you're going to have a very bad day." He scraped the edge of the wand along my spine all the way down to my sore rear. I hated to admit it to myself, but I enjoyed that warning and the calm control he had over the situation. Even the ache of every muscle in my body felt horrifically good when touched by him.

Returning my composure to our little act, and fearful of how he might retaliate, I softened my voice. "Please, Master, forgive me." The last thing I needed was a cold shower or no bath at all. And I definitely didn't want him to keep me from classes for the day.

"You need to earn my forgiveness, slave." He nudged my backside with the black stick, warning of a shock. At least it wasn't a straight-out cattle prod.

How exactly would I earn said forgiveness? As ordered, my sore knees glid over cold carpet as I crawled into the other room with the tub and got into the steaming water. It was slightly hotter than my preference, but complaining might land me in cold baths in the foreseeable future.

Soon after I got in, I felt his hands on my sore shoulders, gently scrubbing with a silky, coconut-scented lather. If not for the relief of the strained muscles, I would have found the gesture of bathing me like a pet annoying until the moment his sudsy palms worked their way down to my tender breasts. That sensation I remembered from our shower together.

I began to relax into the dedicated massage and the slippery sensation of his thumb circling my rosy nipples as he scrubbed me. Not that I wanted him to know I enjoyed this.

That touch continued downward. "Legs spread," he ordered.

Without hesitation, I obeyed the command, feeling the ache of muscles that had been pushed too far the day before. If it felt half as good as some of the other things he'd done, then I would be soothed. Of course, there was also a risk of discomfort, but this event didn't seem to be headed that way. As he stepped around beside me and leaned forward, I got a good, long look at his handsome face and dark eyes. Older, yes, at thirty or so, but still fantastically handsome.

At his age, he should have had a trophy wife. One he cheated on, as some of the men my mom had dated. I knew this Master who currently claimed me wasn't married, though. After seeing his father with my mother, maybe it repulsed him to deal with greedy women. Or maybe none tolerated his actions.

This time, he lowered a white cloth into the water before lifting my leg to gently wash it, moving all the way up to my thigh, squeezing the sudsy water from it as he went. This went on for a while. After he'd taken his time cleaning both my legs, he let the cloth sink into the water and began stroking his adept fingers along my slit, then spreading my sensitive folds to tease and cleanse the area.

Should this have been humiliating? Maybe if I weren't so exhausted or in such a state of physical pain. My eyes were wide as his connected to them.

That touch sent a different heat straight into my nub that begged for more of him. It desired the pleasure he'd provided. Forget tenderness and care for muscles. It needed the velvety soft feel of his cock as it entered my pained core. He must have known by the way his fingers continued to glide the area, teasing both sides of my nub as he washed away the evidence of our long night of the humiliating fucking.

My fingernails dug into the lip of the tub as his motions became more pleasing. He knew exactly how to rile my need, and he did do just that as he plunged into me, bringing an arch to my back as my full body responded to the curl and depth of his fingers. He'd done it so suddenly, so shockingly fast, that I couldn't remain composed in my response.

One would think he might gloat at the sight of me unable to hinder the quivering moan. He merely scanned my expression, stone-faced and unreadable. That in-and-out continued, sometimes speeding, sometimes slowing, but always aware of my physical response and desperation.

He'd brought me to the edge faster than I ever brought myself, but that precipice was the only place he seemed to want me to be. The pleasure teased at me further when he stilled his hand but dipped down to take my breast into his mouth.

My responding tremble sent ripples through the water, my hips bucking upward to meet his hand so I could finalize that orgasm I'd been taunted with. As it began to surface, I clung to his head, digging my fingertips into his hair as my body fully arched out from the water.

He just needed to let me have this piece of gratification. After all, he'd tormented and exhausted me. I'd willingly let him humiliate and shame me, so I would take this without asking. The cry I released shook with the convulsing satisfaction of the experience.

He continued his nipple play, slurping and even scraping with teeth before he released it. "I see I'm going to need to order a chastity belt to teach you a bit of self-control and patience."

Chapter Fourteen: Rewards

After the self-proclaimed Master made me a breakfast of oatmeal, he had me kneel in front of where he sat angled outward from the new, tall kitchen table with metal legs bolted to the floor. He lowered a bowl in front of his fancy shoes, only inches from the fronts of my knees I'd lowered onto.

He may not have permitted me clothes, but at least he gave me a spoon. I took the bowl and spoon in my hands.

"The bowl stays where I put it," he snapped. His scrutinizing stare roved over me with a lack of interest in my nudity.

I supposed wealthy men had plenty of options, and my imperfect curves weren't up to par with the women he was used to, whose life goals included doing anything to be trophy wives.

I didn't want to be anything like my mother, so why did his lack of interest cut so deep? Maybe it was the number of times he used me like a receptacle for his seed. The sensual way he'd touched me, and how he exposed a vulnerable side I refused to reveal to any other person.

My responding glare upward ended with the shock wand beneath my chin.

"I see I'll need to add a few items to the chastity belt order to deal with your bad posture and poor attitude." His tone had shifted after the bath.

The man I'd detested for years returned with full force. With his free hand, he began to type on the screen of his phone.

I grit my teeth, even more resentful of his insult. How could anyone possibly have good posture or a delighted response to eating on the floor?

The tip of the stick beneath my chin prodded upward, threatening a painful jolt if I didn't move as it directed me.

His coy delight at my immediate worry caused a familiar response within me. I loved that twisted joy in his expression. The way the edges of his lips twitched as I obediently followed the wand's guidance. My back straightened and my chest angled upward. Even as sore as my muscles were, he would receive my obedience.

The stick tickled to the very edge of my chin, tilting my head upward. "That's so much better, slave." His words came out so sexy, so in control. Praising me as his gaze trailed down to where the need already built between my legs.

Could he see the desire he'd stirred within me with nothing more than a threat with a torture stick and his sadistic smile?

Fuck me! This excitement from his threat had my chest quivering. Our eyes met, his searching the depths of my soul.

His brows rose. "Thank me."

The ability to speak evaded me. Breathing in a controlled manner seemed hard enough. The wand trailed down from my chin, passing my chest before he leaned forward to tap the end against my nub. Even then, I only wanted to get lost in his dark eyes and the thick lips that slightly parted. I could remember that expression numerous times in the short period he'd decided to upend my life, sometimes preparing to praise me. Or at least with a bit of joy in what was to come.

The painful zap between my legs woke my ability to respond. After a jolt forward, I cried, "Thank you." I took in a deep breath, finishing the response. "Master." I resumed the upright position.

"You're welcome, slave." He placed his evil shocking wand on the table. "You may eat after you hold proper posture."

I returned to the stance that he preferred, scooping up oatmeal and eating in a posture no woman would concern herself with. And while that may have annoyed me, the way he enjoyed the sight gave me reason to want to be the object he planned for me to be for the next month. And at the sight of the bulge in front of me, it seemed I had plenty of control over his reaction to me.

After eating every bit of bland porridge, I lowered the spoon into the empty bowl. When I tilted my head upward to him, he still watched me with judgment.

Extending his hand to my lip, he leaned downward. I could already imagine him demanding I unclasp his pants and free his manhood, so he could endlessly fuck my mouth.

"If you can't eat without making a mess, I won't bother with giving you a spoon." His thumb wiped my lower lip.

Rude. I doubted I'd made a mess of myself at all. More likely, he only said that to get a response from me. If it had come from my ex, an argument would have followed. Only torment would come from an attempt to quarrel with this Master.

He sat upright in his seat. "I want you spread out on the table so I can breed that pretty little cunt."

Not that he actually intended to knock me up, but the statement reminded me that I'd missed my alarm for my birth control pill yesterday evening. Just the thought of pregnancy had me near panicking.

His eyes narrowed as he awaited my next action.

"I need to take my pill...Master." At least I tacked on his title in time.

His head cocked to the side. There wasn't the usual punishment or threat for me speaking without permission. Instead, his inquisitive study of me lingered until I had to look downward to my hands. Maybe he expected me to say more.

I began, "My birth control—"

"Is that something you want, slave?" he asked.

The question seemed beyond stupid. The pill wasn't a want of mine; it was a necessity. It decreased the risk of the next month leading to an unwanted pregnancy. And I wasn't like women who sought out men like him to knock me up.

"I need it," I replied. A conversation might have been essential if it was with someone I planned to date, but he wasn't a casual boyfriend, nor was birth control something I considered a conversation piece.

"You don't need it. You want it."

"Neither of us wants a child added to this arrangement," I retorted. I didn't want to look at him during this discussion. I didn't want it to *be* a discussion. But when the wand prodded my neck and pushed my chin upward, I had no choice.

"Things you want are rewards. Rewards must be earned." Calculation laced his conquering smirk. "My seed is going to be leaking from you at all hours of the day. It's up to you whether or not you are rewarded by not being impregnated with my child. Get on the table and perhaps I can be swayed to reward you."

This was just another piece in his game to permit me to graduate. Even as part of the arrangement, his manner felt more menacing than it should have. As though he'd truly found a way to sink claws into me.

This expectation felt like the most worrisome thing to date. I didn't know why, but something about the hungry set of his jaw and his relaxed posture unnerved me. A false calm shadowed his expression as he awaited me to stand in front of him.

Chapter Fifteen: Table Time

My achy muscles fought against me as I rose. A motor hummed low, drawing my attention to the tabletop that currently lowered. The metal legs bolted to the floor were suspicious, but knowing the height of the table adjusted made me realize this wasn't for dining. And the upper surface looked like grayed wood worn smooth, like it was a set piece for a medieval era film.

When the archaic table stopped at hip height, the Master tapped it with the wand. "You may have your precious pills every day after table-time." He stroked his flattened hand over the surface with pride before leaning to the edge, where several screws and black curved strips of metal waited for a purpose I feared discovering.

"Table-time?" My heart pounded in my chest. Not with excitement, but with horror. Horror at the dance of light in his irises as he drank in my shocked expression.

Of course he wanted me to feel this way. He wanted me to be at his will. But he definitely didn't want a child with me, so no matter the threat, it wouldn't be so horrific he would refuse me my pill.

His keen study caught my every tiny facial twitch. "Table-time is our special time with each other." He stood and wrapped his hands around my waist, lifting me onto the edge of the table.

I did nothing to stop him, but part of me still wanted to run away. "Does *special* mean I'll be inescapably bound to that device?" I asked.

His white teeth beamed past his malevolent grin. "Special means whatever I want it to mean." He let me know the conversation ended when his hands wrapped around my wrists and guided me to lie backward with a force I easily submitted to.

No matter what, he would have me on this table, just as he'd had me in front of my boyfriend or with the movers in the room. I would accept his term of *special* in exchange for the ability to finish university.

With my back to the cool surface, he focused his attention on my positioning. The bulge of his manhood already pressed against my core as he adjusted me a few inches to the left.

The man who'd been willing to hold a conversation no longer remained. This Master had a mission that currently involved a half circle metal piece he brought above my head.

Table-time. Special time. Did I really want to be trapped on this device that had been designed for his twisted enjoyment?

I could buy a morning-after pill every day for the next month. Better yet, I could place them in my pack. While I got carried away with everything I could do instead of being bolted to a table, he placed the curved metal on my neck.

"That's my good little slave." His cock ground against my sensitive core as he leaned against me and reached for something. "I won't even gag you this time."

I still didn't know how much of this terrifying endeavor was an act of his. Nor where his slight shifts were due to sadism or simply loving my response to his worrisome statements and manner.

He placed a screw at one end of the piece of metal binding he'd positioned over my neck. Why not a collar to clip to the tabletop? That would be less involved and wouldn't feel so horrific. I wanted to make my argument against being bolted to the table, but a gag and the shock wand might be his only response.

I'd probably given him more leverage over me with my request for birth control. I would've been better off pretending to want to get knocked up by him. That would have been the most effective way of ensuring I got my pill easily.

The metal that held my neck to the table wasn't tight, but if I moved, it would catch my skin. After a few more screws guaranteed my head was secured, the wrist bindings were put into place next, trapping my wrists at level with the top of my head. Sure, I had freedom in my legs for now, but when would that end?

Maybe it was the terror of the situation that had my heart racing and a need steadily increasing where his groin bumped my core. Even through my worry, that sensation began to take over. I could do nothing about what was to come of being beneath him, but I could hope this *special time* together included gratification instead of cruel punishment.

Moving my wrists against the metal proved these restraints were screwed in too tight for any give. Anything could go wrong. What if a fire broke out? Unlikely, yes, but he couldn't heroically rip the metal from the table if there was an emergency.

"Master," I said meekly now that I'd foolishly let him trap me into this predicament.

His brow furrowed as he placed the screwdriver to the side. "Is there something you need, slave? Because if it's only a want, I'll gag you and punish you for every word you choose to speak without necessity."

I began to doubt he cared about my worry. Maybe my need to be certain of safety would be deemed as nothing more than a want to him. He could consider the question as my lack of trust in his ability to keep me bound here without serious harm to my person.

No. That would be foolish to risk.

One month. I only needed to keep him happy for that long. I could leave all this behind me, as well as any dependence on a man for financial stability.

After several seconds of silence, he returned upright, guiding his hands along my sides and downward to my waist. "Good girl," he said. "But you've still done several terrible things to be disciplined for."

Chapter Sixteen: Another Chance

I hated the expression on his face as he spoke of punishment. The seriousness of his tone. Even the glint in his eyes added to my spiraling angst.

"And I don't think you will be in any condition to go to classes today." He picked up the wand that he'd already shocked me with several times.

Our agreement included finishing university without issue. He couldn't do this to me, especially not with the genuine intent written on his face.

I raised my head as best I could, which wasn't much before the metal confining me hindered further movement. "If I have to do anything else for you, I will get my classes and graduate."

With a glower downward, he had the wand to my nub and zapped me—painfully.

I cried out, jolting and hitting my Adam's apple against the metal bar entrapping me.

"Finishing classes is a reward." He released the painful current again, possibly stronger. "Receiving your precious birth control is a reward." He'd morphed into someone unrecognizable, acting excessively cruel without justification.

"You—"

Another painful shock had me jerking against the restraints that dug into my flesh.

"Speaking is a reward."

"Fuck yo—"

The next shock lasted several seconds and had me fighting beneath the restraints even more, chafing my wrists.

"One more reply without permission, and you'll be gagged." He tossed the wand beside me and dug in his trousers pocket, pulling out the electric nipple clamps.

Now I sobbed; each breath its own punishment as my movements caused more pain. The next hiccup stopped me from further talking. He was a monster. An absolute, horrible, horrible monster. University for torture? This was the way our agreement would go? Birth control in exchange for this?

His crotch pressed against me as he leaned forward to clamp one nipple, and then the other. They were still sore and hurt worse than the night before. With my sensitivity and the lack of release earlier, he got a bodily reaction of excitement out of me. And I hated him all the more for his ability to do that to me.

In our previous sexual encounters, he proved gentle, which made me trust this wouldn't happen. Not now. Now I wondered if he only planned to keep me locked away and bound and assault me on his whim. He'd already told my ex that I would be taking time off.

"That's better, little slave. I don't want to have to take away the breeding table. You wouldn't get your birth control or get to go to class."

What the fuck? Breeding table? Did he consider this torment to be a reward as well? I would need to act appreciative of this? It wasn't like I would bother hiding my scowl.

Now the shock went to my breasts, causing me to jolt worse than before. Not just briefly, and even after a short reprieve, he increased the strength and did it again.

"If you plan to act like an angry little brat and aren't appreciative, I can take it away." He raised the end of the wand between my legs.

"Tha–Tha–" The word hardly came out given the pain in my throat and fear. I finally croaked, "thank you, Master."

He'd clearly won. He'd set this up to win. And no matter what, there would be pain, or there would be worse suffering.

"That's my good girl," he cooed. "Learning already."

If he hoped praise made this feel better, he was wrong. In no way was this acceptable. Once he freed me of this breeding table, I wouldn't let him do it again. He wouldn't stop me from birth control or going to class. But no way in hell would I piss him off while he had me trapped in such an inescapable way.

When pressure landed at my core, I jolted, terrified of the shock to come. It didn't happen, though.

"Keep being good for me, little one, and you won't be shocked again." His fingers stroked my nub, causing a pleasure I desperately fought against. I could be *good* without falling for the trap of near orgasm or worse; being forced to have one.

It took everything within me not to speak my mind. And with as tight as my jaw clenched from my anger, having the gag might have been a relief to my teeth.

"How about I show you what good slaves receive?" he asked. "What would you like for me to do to you?"

Was this permission to speak? A wish of mine to be granted? "Let me off this table...Please, Master."

"Oh, but little slave, you want your birth control, right? And to go to class tomorrow?" He spread my folds and continued to stroke that perfect spot that made my body react with need, taking in heavy breaths as he looked down on my exposed core.

The threat of holding birth control and a university degree hostage was its own cruel torment. As was the way he switched from punishment to pleasure. I refused to look at him.

"You know..." one of his fingers dipped into me. "I know you are supposed to graduate with honors by your own hard work. I respect that." His digit pumped into me, adding to the sensation of the pressure against my nub. "I don't want you to lose that, especially given your near perfect attendance. But I still expect you to earn it instead of using a rich old man for his money and his sway as you did."

My eyes met his. The certainty in his stare bore the dare to doubt his power. And while I'd resolved to tell him to fuck off the moment he freed me from this table, what hit the hardest was how he basically equated my actions to those of my mother. I was nothing like her. I didn't want anything for free.

He'd attacked me with more than threats to win this battle. He used my unwillingness to be like my mother as a weapon against me. And knowing my detest of her lifestyle, he planned to exploit that as well.

Enduring him would be the only way to guarantee my success and my pride. Being his *good little slave* for a month would be painful, but doable. And once I graduated and left, he couldn't accuse me of being anything like my mother. Sure, sex was involved, but not to receive anything current or in the future. Not like so many women using their bodies for gain.

I forced a pleasant response. I could prove him wrong in his judgment of me and make this month as comfortable as possible. "Yes, Master. I want my birth control and to graduate with honors." It took everything within me to hold a sincere expression of humility when I added, "Forgive me for not considering those as rewards."

His hand movements were slow, creating the need for release, but he'd built my bliss to a near explosion and refused me gratification already today. His expression held the sort of charm that didn't suggest a man using coercion and shame to have a personal fuck-toy.

"How about I give you another chance? If you're really good, I might even reward you with different restraints for our special table time. Would you like that?"

What a stupid question. Of course I preferred that. Only a fool wouldn't accept the offer. I could still secretly detest him, but this made the situation tolerable.

"Yes, Master...thank you."

"You're welcome, little one." The table motor hummed, and, as it lowered, he got on his knees.

I hesitated in my response, not daring to move too quickly against the metal imprisoning me. I didn't need it rubbing my skin raw. Yet something magnetic about him had my head slightly tilted, so my stare met his as he pushed my thighs further apart and his face closed in on my core.

I didn't want him down there. I didn't want anyone down there. I couldn't respond as I wanted to; I had to submit. At least I had to appear to submit. Obeying his wishes wasn't a loss when it involved self-respect and using my own actions to shape the way he treated me.

Chapter Seventeen: Relax

One kiss close to my core.
Another.

Two more, even closer.

The Master's flattened tongue tracing my slit.

Warm air added to the mix and sent heat through me. He shouldn't have felt this good, but the slow and teasing caresses with his tongue were just enough pressure to have me desperate for slightly more.

I could free myself and have this. I'd gained something else from accepting the agreement. In making him happy, I won in the end. He could never insult me with the claim that I'd used someone's wealth to get what I wanted.

Next came the suction as he focused his attention on that sensitive bundle of nerves.

My responding gasp and quiver had him dedicating himself more to my slow building climax. With my neck sore, and few options for what would happen, I chose to lay back and let this slow journey to bliss come.

Would he bring me close to release again as he did in the bath? I could feel it teasing me with the promise. I let him have the control he demanded. His slowing suction and strokes of his tongue meant he felt my reaction and planned to steer it.

"Master," I moaned the whisper. I didn't simply want it. I needed it from him. He would like that. It was a bit of praise to his bloated ego.

He hummed with questioning but didn't stop.

"Please."

His next hum came as a chuckle. His motions slowed even more, torturing me by drawing out the arrival of my orgasm. He wouldn't let this happen on my timescale.

My mental energy went to the feel of what he was doing. To the imagined passion in another place and time. Unfortunately, not to a different person. He still lingered in the fantasy I created in my mind.

As my enjoyment continued to grow, despite his decreased pace, the door hissed open from the apartment entry to my right. Now my spacious open layout to the dining room and kitchen didn't feel so charming at the sight of someone stepping inside.

I feared my ex returned to see me before our class began. This man was too tall, and when I turned my head, I recognized him as one of the movers from yesterday. Even in the humiliation of being seen, I still didn't lose the nearing climax.

One month. Just one month needed to prove I wasn't a selfish woman who lived on rich men.

The Master stopped and kissed my inner thigh before rising to his feet. "You aren't allowed to see what they're bringing for you."

While I should have feared retaliation for what he deemed a misbehavior worthy of the shock wand or clamps, his voice held humor.

I looked to the ceiling before a careful glance to him.

"Request my forgiveness," he ordered, still with calmness.

"Please, Master, forgive me for my curiosity." I may have known he had a ridiculous demand for nothing more than to see who would spy on me while laid out, but I had no choice but to accept that this mover-man would watch.

The Master rose, now using his hand to add to the need for release. His focus went to the other room. He reached behind him before retrieving something small and black. When he brought it toward my face, I already knew what it was. A blindfold.

Arguing would be of no use. This would happen in front of someone, and I had to accept that truth as he unfolded the wide cloth and placed it over my eyes. He was gentle as he tied it, careful not to pull my hair.

"Oh, how good you're behaving for me," he purred.

Now, as blackness took hold, I had to rely on my other senses to gather what he planned next.

His zipper sounded, alerting me to the event about to take place.

Pants rustled, bumping against me as they lowered.

A warm hand explored my left thigh, sending a tickle along my outer leg before a long, quiet pause. Both angst and longing swirled through me, battling as I awaited his next action.

His manhood slid into my tender and drenched folds. Even his breathing during the easy push created further want to be fucked passionately. A desperation for the release he'd worked me up to. Instead of instant bliss, the ache for it hovered as he pumped into me.

Each rock of his cock into me had my need steadily rising. He'd already had me ready to explode. Now he drew it out for a while.

"Cum for me while I breed your perfect cunt, little slave," he ordered, before leaning forward to remove the clamps. "Let me feel you drink me into your womb."

Something about his statement excited me. I knew it held no true intent to impregnate me, but the idea remained exciting at the moment.

When his mouth latched onto my breast, bliss overtook me.

My release came with an arch to my back and a need to grab onto something instead of being trapped on the table. And I clamped tighter around his cock when he shoved hilt-deep and hot seed blast into me.

Kisses to my chest continued the passion, and he didn't pull out. He held in place with his weight on me.

Knowing he most likely expected appreciation, I said, "Thank you, Master."

"You're so very welcome, little one." Our connection broke and stole the warmth he'd provided. "I need to help them. You just relax here and soak in my cum."

I wanted to beg to be released, or for the blindfold to be removed, but I doubted he would accept. This was what he wanted. My submission to him made his arrogant ego happy.

All I could say was, "Yes, Master," with forced delight in my tone.

When he left me trapped on the table, I could only wonder what might be happening in the spacious entry area. Steps and movement came from there, even voices at times.

After a while, someone used a drill. That sound worried me. The master didn't seem like the type to hang pictures on the wall. With this bondage device as a table, I didn't want to find out what he deemed to be furniture for entertaining guests.

The steps that closed in on me didn't end with a caress of fingertips, rather, the sound of clunky metal to my right. The strain of weight creaked, so I could only assume someone stood on a ladder. Affirmation of my assumption came when I heard more drilling from up high. At least it wasn't something directly above me.

The person worked there for a while, most likely gawking down at my nude form, waiting helplessly. I still heard the other movements further in the open area that once had charm and elegant furnishings.

Whoever drilled something into the ceiling left, and I remained for a while, chilled as though the overheated men must have decided to turn off the heater to keep themselves cool. Never mind concerning themselves with whether I would become too cold. Slaves didn't complain, their needs came last.

Chapter Eighteen: Wonderful Things

By the time the next light taps of steps came my way, I'd finally mastered my over-awareness of the frigid conditions. Now came a warm hand to my stomach, causing a gasp of overwhelming relief. He'd left me to this suffering long enough that his touch alone brought joy to me.

"Have you missed me, little slave?"

I swallowed, and I tried to control my quiver. "Yes, Master."

More movement came from the other room. Crumpling paper or packaging, if I heard the noise correctly.

His hand traced up to one of my sore breasts, taking my right nipple between his fingers. The pain I expected didn't come. This hadn't been a punishing grip.

"You look so good. I can hardly stop myself from fucking you." He switched his attention to the other breast, fondling it as well. "But we both need to wait and be rewarded after you open a few of your gifts."

After his arousing touch ended, he leaned over me, and I felt the heat of his bare chest that lowered to mine briefly. Luckily, he quickly went to work on the metal that planted my neck on the table.

The sound of the screw turning couldn't pass fast enough, and I worried that, at any moment, he might change his mind about letting me off the table. But I'd kept him happy after our little spat earlier. I could continue to keep him satisfied with my behavior. It may have been annoying to stroke his ego instead of being truthful, but it kept a much-needed peace to ensure I endured this coming month.

After my neck, he removed the metal restraints on my wrists as well. Finally. freedom from that nightmare.

I sat upright, aching, but ready to go to the bathroom and get his cum cleared off of me.

A prod to my thigh ended with a powerful shock.

I jolted on the edge of the table, almost falling forward.

"I've been lenient and permitted you a new start to the day, but don't think you can do whatever you wish." He removed the prodding tip of the wand from my leg.

Obey. Keep him happy. Do whatever I needed to do in order to earn a good and respectable life.

"Forgive me, Master," I breathed.

"Of course." His lips pressed to my temple. The change seemed so rapid it was near unbelievable. But men like him were always pacified by being in control. This person kissing me and speaking softly felt nothing like someone who would easily shock me for a simple act of sitting upright.

He leaned behind me and untied the blindfold. "I've gotten you several things that I know you'll love."

With the cloth gone, I captured the glistening of his eyes that searched mine. I could keep him like this, excited and without the need to shock or hurt me. I'd be tolerating his annoying expectations, but this seemed easily manageable.

"Thank you, Master." My smile felt weak, but not quite forced. But I did feel a true gratitude toward him for freeing me from the table and removing the blindfold. Sadly, even given this relief, my expectations of men hadn't really lowered from the days with my cheating ex.

I glanced around in a new silence. "Are we alone, Master?"

"That's of no concern to you, slave," he said sternly. "Know your place, or I'll have to discipline you."

Of course. Only bring up things that are considered needs.

I bit the inside of my lower lip, not knowing how to address the awkwardness of an inability to ask simple questions.

He hooked his finger beneath my chin. "There are so many wonderful things I got you. Let's not ruin this joy we share by forcing me to punish you."

I nodded. "Thank you...Master." It was a bit harder to say this time.

"Come now, slave." He took my hand and pulled me upright onto stiff legs. I would have assumed he intended to make me crawl, but he didn't. He wanted my hand in his as he led me onward.

When he stepped out of my way, I caught sight of a crimson lounger with a seat shaped at the angle of a high-heeled shoe. The top ended at hip height, and the lower area faced away from the far corner with plenty of distance from the corner wall that he could bend me over the high back and fuck me on it if he wanted. It may have been surrounded by white bags and boxes like a Christmas tree, but my attention went to the next worrisome furnishing.

Toward the center of the living area was a pale, round baluster that must have been made of one large piece of stone. The top had the diameter of a small plate and reached around hip height. The most unnerving thing about it was the metal ring at the center that partially protruded from the top. There were also a few of those same fasteners located along the sides of the bottom, which increased in girth and had medieval carving. Maybe it had once adorned a gothic home before being used as a piece of furniture I had no desire to become acquainted with.

My head turned its direction, still taking in the large stone creation while the Master led me to the red lounger. He sat and pulled me down onto his lap, facing sideways, though I still had eyes on the pillar.

"Your attention remains on me, slave." A poke to my lower back informed me of the punishing wand he could use if he chose to do so. At least he didn't treat me as he had earlier during the repeated shocks. He'd chosen not to punish me for such stupid reasons, even if the threat to do so continued.

"I'm sorry, Master. I..." I may have turned my head to him to satisfy his need to be the center of my attention, but my thoughts lingered on what would happen at the gothic baluster.

The windows may have let morning light in, but I figured out the reason for some of the drilling had been black curtains along the wall that, when closed, would block all natural light.

"You're excited, I know. But I don't want you overwhelmed and focused on too many new things when there are presents to be opened." He bent down to retrieve one of the white packages. He normally would have forced me to kneel near his feet instead of straining himself to get a present for me. I couldn't believe how much he'd changed over my simple responses to satisfy him. And I had no desire to return to my knees and kneel at his feet or to crawl.

Of course, being seated on his lap and coddled felt a bit like he pretended to be a doting daddy. But far better than the hostile owner's attitude or his coerciveness upon arrival.

After retrieving a medium-sized tall bag, he returned upright and held it in front of me.

"Thank you." I hoped he didn't catch the tremble in my hand as I took the package. What gift would he give to me, given the additions he'd made to my home?

Anticipation seemed absurd, and I wasn't overjoyed to receive something from him. I needed to know what he considered a gift for me, and I also needed to hold a genuine delight in my response to it.

His left palm lowered to my thigh to rest, but he leaned forward to kiss my shoulder as I opened the package.

The decorative white tissue paper hissed as I pushed it to the side, revealing a red leather strap.

He hummed against my shoulder as I pulled it from the package. It seemed he enjoyed giving it to me, whatever it happened to be. When I'd lifted the flexible item with numerous buckles, it became obvious this was no single strip of leather, but a network of straps.

How the fuck was I supposed to beam in response to such an atrocious piece of fetish stuff? It might have been an outfit or possibly some sort of sick gear to bind my body at strange angles. I had no clue.

Chapter Nineteen: Do You Like It

"Do you like it?" he asked.

The words were spoken as though he expected me to know what he'd given me. And the tone held the assumption that I had a desire to have the things someone playing as a slave might like.

"I..." A thank you would be expected first, or maybe a yes. "Thank you, Master, yes."

He chuckled against the back of my shoulder. "Do you know what it is?"

"I..." Of course I didn't. "No, Master."

"Let me help you put it on." He took the strappy thing and bent forward to hold it in front of my feet.

I already knew to lift one and then the other before being ordered to. He worked it up my legs where the lowest strips rested at the underwear line of my lower rear. The bundle fell into place with straps along my sides, then to the triangles that framed my breasts and then went up the back of my neck like a halter.

I cringed at the sight of my breasts lined in such a way. This felt worse than being naked. He adjusted the various buckles to tighten the leather item and pulled some of the rings to test the tightness. A thicker strap ran the length of my spine, and this one he firmly tugged between my shoulder blades where the other leather connected to it.

His erection pushed against my outer thigh as his tug brought me closer to his body. My slit remained exposed and available for whatever he planned to do to me. And by the hardness grinding against me, I had an idea of what would happen next.

"I never expected this could look so amazing," he purred. "Do you like it?" He yanked the back strap with a force that had my breasts pinched and my cheek to his face.

"Yes, Master," I breathed. "Thank you for the wonderful gift, Master."

"That's my very good girl." He gripped my head and turned it so our mouths connected. The closeness and the firm squeeze that landed on my breast built the need for his touch again. No matter how embarrassing this moment may have been, my body didn't care in the least.

"You make this so difficult for me to resist pounding into your perfect little cunt." His next breath came out with a tremble. It wasn't something I expected I had any control over. I'd simply tried to ensure his happiness to keep things tolerable.

He readjusted beneath me, letting me feel his cock against my thigh as he reached a foot toward a box with a gift bag stacked atop it, pulling them both closer. The bag fell our direction, and a bit of matching red leather peeked out.

"Open your next gift, slave."

I leaned forward, twisting as I bent to reach the bag. His strong hold went down between my thighs, controlling my movement as I sat upright, guiding me to face outward on his lap with my legs spreading as he also pulled me back against his cock.

I took out scarlet cuffs to match the halter. Wrists or ankles? I would find out soon enough. His gentle squeeze of my inner legs ensured me of that.

I obediently raised and lowered one into the hand he extended in front of my stomach. Just to see it so close to my core made me wish he could relieve the ache boiling over before whatever torment he had planned. He worked the imprisoning device open with ease before wrapping my small wrist and securing it. He did this with both wrists.

"Thank you, Master," I obediently said with as much appreciation in my tone as I could muster.

"And the box, now, little slave." Something about how he'd said it didn't sit well, but that only added to my bizarrely foolish anticipation.

He held an unnatural excitement to me this way. Like an adolescent boy, hardly able to control his urges. Fortunately, he'd already fucked me fairly recently, so he wasn't overpowered by a need to claim me roughly.

I again bent forward, this time scooping up the cube that felt heavier than the other items. This didn't feel as innocent. Not to say any were innocent, but this had a darker concern fill me. Maybe this would be the last present for now, and hopefully, my sudden dread could pass.

I opened it to reveal an item matching the deep red color of the other leather items. It must have been a collar, but several inches wide and inflexibly thick. It would probably control posture with precision. Nothing about its design suggested comfort, definitely not the large ring in the front designed to be used for attaching a chain lead, or the small ridges outlining the curve beneath where the soft skin beneath my chin would rest.

Any excitement and anticipation fled me. Horrified by the thought of wearing this, I didn't even notice when he reached upward to my tight grip of the collar. The silent demand didn't register.

He kissed the back of my neck and let out a soft hum of joy. A noise that seemed oblivious to my awareness of this as a humiliating device of torture. "This is going to be your last chance to refuse me and leave my apartment, little slave." He spoke the words loud, perhaps knowing the pounding in my ears dulled everything around me.

Not ready to let him put the collar on me, I pulled it up to my chest and away from his expectant hand.

Deep down, I knew I didn't have a choice in the matter. Not when so much was at stake. Not if proving I was nothing like my conniving mother could result.

Rejecting him meant I endured the humiliation he'd already subjected me to with nothing to show. Could I walk away after that? That alone seemed foolish. I'd already invested myself in this. What more could he possibly do to me? This was another act of his.

Sure, he'd pretended to plan a torture session when he had me trapped on the barbaric table. In the end, there was no pain beyond the initial shocks. Shame for being on display to the other men. But this Master's bark proved to be far worse than his bite.

Besides, I already figured out how to keep him content and nice.

Chapter Twenty: The Master

The Master

I loved that initial fear, but it passed far too quickly. Her arrogance still shaped her reaction to me. Even the way her responses held their own conceited ridicule. But whether she admitted it or not, she'd lost this game before I arrived in the apartment.

How many years did I tolerate her bitchy attitude during the times she stayed in my father's home? Too fucking many.

Yet in all the times she acted like a bitch, I knew the flash in her eyes. The one that had basically begged for me to break into her room and ravish her. The one I tried to ignore, so I didn't end up with someone as despicable as her mother bleeding me dry.

Given how much money my father spent on this woman, she'd practically been bought and paid for. She was an added bonus alongside his fortune and the successful company I inherited.

"Turn and face me," I ordered.

She turned immediately, her large bright eyes flashing that same need to be ravished. But they also held a triumph that needed to be crumpled. "Yes, Master."

Such confidence in herself accompanied those words. Even the way her leg lifted in a self-assured manner before she straddled my lap. More like her swindling slut mother than the submissive she thought she pretended to be.

The insincerity would be met with force.

She clutched the collar to her breasts, which were nicely outlined and lifted in the matching harness she wore. Her lips parted as she pretended to think about the matter, but we both knew her pride wouldn't let her refuse me.

This time, I gave her a firm glare when I plucked the collar from her hold. "We can end this now, or you can choose to stay?"

The camera nearby captured my clear words. She could never say she hadn't agreed to this.

I removed the dangling small padlock and opened the buckle to spread the collar between us, ready for her to lean forward to accept it. I knew I had her. She'd loved the pain and pleasure. Her need to be ruled over by me was unlike anything I'd ever experienced with any other woman. She could hide it all she wanted, but I knew a masochist lurked beneath her surface. A sub who needed to be punished and ruled over without any say whatsoever.

She stared down to the awaiting collar with too much confidence.

"If you agree to this arrangement, I'm going to punish you until you can't walk."

Her doe eyes fluttered. She doubted me, or rather, she thought she could control me with her arrogant charms. She thought acting like her mother for a little while might pacify me.

I huffed at the thought of what this meant to her. One month, nothing more. I would let her earn her degree and feel accomplished. Let her feel like more than a trophy with a belly swollen with my child, wholly obedient to me and desperate for my affection. A perfect prize on my arm, but nothing like the vipers who attempted to trick me into a loveless marriage.

My gaze flicked from hers to the collar, then back to her. "You're going to beg every single day. I'm going to fuck and humiliate you in front of my friends and colleagues. I'm going to breed your womb without mercy time and time and time again. And when you are too pregnant to obey my orders, I'll have you bound on your back so I can fuck you even more. Or you can get the fuck out now."

More challenge sparked within her. A need to prove she wasn't weak; that she simply called my bluff. Only, I hadn't bluffed about a single bit of my intent for her.

"I'm not afraid, Master," she said, keeping the same attitude she'd had this entire time. That sultry voice used was just like any woman who hoped to lie to me.

I may have ignored her little act of calling me Master without sincerity, but not after this collar locked into place.

She leaned forward, pressing her neck to the collar, her harnessed chest quivering with every rushed breath. And she already looked like the perfect woman to be waiting with her legs spread wide for the ravenous pounding she would receive every time I desired to have her.

"Lift your hair," I ordered.

With her arms raised to lift her hair, I couldn't help but stare at her waiting breasts as I cinched the collar into place, snapping the small lock with triumph.

"Now then, slave." I didn't bother to hide my satisfaction as I dug beneath the lounger and wrapped my fist around the waiting padlock. The one to keep her in place while I reminded her of her role as my slave.

I hooked the curved end into the metal ring on the front of her collar. "Lock this to the stay on the top of the post while you are facing that camera." I pointed to the camera that had been installed above the table she'd been restrained to earlier.

Doubt finally crept into her expression, but there was no backing out now.

Don't miss out!

Visit the website below and you can sign up to receive emails whenever Maebel Credence publishes a new book. There's no charge and no obligation.

https://books2read.com/r/B-A-SJRX-XVVUC

BOOKS 2 READ

Connecting independent readers to independent writers.

Also by Maebel Credence

The Heir
Dominated by the Heir

Standalone
Armon's Revenge
Neighborly Attraction
Noah's Ark